BLOODY AMBASSADORS

A NOTE ON THE AUTHOR

Sean O'Brien lives in County Waterford. He is married and has two daughters. *Bloody Ambassadors* is his first book, the fruit of many years' research in true crime.

Sean O'Brien

Bloody Ambassadors

POOLBEG

First published 1993 by
Poolbeg Press Ltd
Knocksedan House,
Swords, Co Dublin, Ireland

© Sean O'Brien 1993

The moral right of the author has been asserted.

A catalogue record for this book is available from the British Library.

ISBN 1 85371 232 9

Cover design by Pomphrey Associates
Set by Mac Book Limited in Stone 9.5/12
Printed by The Guernsey Press Company Ltd,
Vale, Guernsey, Channel Islands

This book is for Linda, Roisin and Sinead.

Acknowledgements

In writing this book, I received help from many sources. For their assistance, I wish to thank the staff of the Newspaper Division, New York Public Library, NY; the staff of the Goodell Library, University of Massachusetts, Amherst, Mass.; the staff of the City of Westminster Archives Department, Victoria Library, London; the staff of the British Library, Newspaper Library, London; the staff of the State Library of New South Wales, Sydney, Australia; and the staff of the Alexander Turnbull Library, Wellington, New Zealand.

Nearer home, I owe a debt of gratitude to the staff of the Cork County Library, and for his willing assistance I would like especially to thank County Librarian, Tim Cadogan.

My thanks are also due to Jeanette Woods, as much for deciphering my writing as for her excellent typing. And, finally, I wish to express my deep appreciation to my family for their constant patience and encouragement.

Preface

As a nation we have tended to exile. We probably deserve the sobriquet of the Wandering Irish. In this respect history recorded us as saints and scholars; then Hollywood cast us as priests and policemen. Each view contains its own truths. But the wandering Irish were just as renowned in bootlegging, organised crime and political bribery and corruption. Less well known, perhaps, is the fact that as murderers the Irish exiles hold their own with the very worst.

In the ten murder cases described in the following pages, all the accused were Irish. Of the seven men and three women charged with unlawful killing, five faced prosecution in courts in England, two in America, while the remaining cases were tried in New Zealand, Scotland and West Germany.

As widely diverse as the locations of the murders, were the motivations of the alleged killers and the methods used to destroy the victims. The victims, like the accused murderers, represented both the eminently respected and the socially deprived.

The crimes spanned eras of great change in social conditions, in forensic science and in the very definitions of murder and its punishment, particularly in the offering of the defence of diminished responsibility.

Each of the selected cases took place against a background of sensational publicity which at the time attracted nationwide attention, with two trials—those of William Burke in Edinburgh in 1828 and Dr John Adams in London in 1957—being reported in newspapers throughout the world. Some intriguing element was present in every case; in one way or another, all were dramatic.

Having eliminated what I considered inessential and repetitious material, I hope the drama has survived.

In writing the stories of these ten infamous Irish exiles, I consulted many books. While all were helpful and are included in the bibliography, edited transcripts of six of the trials were also available and they were essential reading. They require special mention: Dr Adams's trial is extensively dealt with in Sybille Bedford's *The Best We Can Do*; the trials of William Burke and Kate Webster appear in the volumes of the excellent series, *Notable British Trials*; Robert Butler's exploits are covered in *The Cumberland Street Tragedy* (no author) and Daniel McFarland's case in AR Cazauran's *The Trial of Daniel McFarland*. The history of Mrs Robinson's case is set out by JMW Yerrington in *The Trial of Sarah Jane Robinson*.

These works proved invaluable to me and I am pleased to acknowledge the fact. Also of enormous help in recounting the four remaining cases were Allen Andrews's treatment of Patrick Byrne's trial in *Intensive Inquiries*; Dr JB Firth's record of the Clements case in *A Scientist Turns to Crime*; Ian Bissitt's account of Frederick Emmett-Dunne's court martial in *Trial at Arms*; and Gaute and Odell's fine study of Charlotte Bryant in *Ladykillers*. For the period relevant to each trial, newspapers were also consulted.

CONTENTS

1

THE WEST PORT MURDERS

William Burke   **Edinburgh, 1828**

In Burke and Hare, Ireland produced two of the world's most infamous murderers. The gruesome activities of the pair in Edinburgh in the late 1820s resulted in the most famous case in Scottish legal history. Numerous melodramas retold their story in barns and village-halls throughout the length of Britain and many authors, from Thomas De Quincey to Dylan Thomas, were fascinated by the theme of their ghoulish crimes.

With each retelling, the details became distorted until eventually many of the facts were lost to legend.

In Edinburgh in 1827, the study of anatomy was so essential and popular at the university's Faculty of Medicine, and at the several other medical schools in the city, that a huge demand was created for dead bodies for dissection. The only lawful supply available to anatomists at the time were the cadavers of criminals who had died either in prison or on the scaffold. But, however sparing they were with limbs and organs, lecturers in anatomy never had enough specimens and supplies dispatched from outside Scotland rarely reached the surgeon's lecture rooms. This was especially true of illegal supplies sent from Ireland.

Bodies shipped through the port of Dublin were

sometimes concealed in barrels of brine but more frequently they were packed in wooden crates. At times, when carried as deck cargo, they were washed overboard but if stowed for safety in a ship's hold, there were other problems to be faced. Even a slight delay at sea because of unfavourable weather conditions meant an advance in putrefaction. The consequent stench when a ship's hatch covers were lifted was all the evidence needed to tell the Glasgow port authorities that they had discovered another consignment of decomposing Irish corpses. Those difficulties, though, were not enough to dissuade some ambitious shippers in Ireland who had developed a flourishing export trade in dead bodies, most of them stolen from Dublin's unprotected cemeteries.

Edinburgh's original grave-robbers were enthusiastic medical students who would quickly dig up a freshly buried corpse for the purpose of study. But those young men were soon frightened away from graveyards by the violence of hardened criminals who turned to grave-robbing as a profitable full-time occupation. Despite their efforts, supplies were declining all the time and "resurrectionists" and body-snatchers were unable to meet the increasing demand, mostly because grave-robbing was becoming a dangerous as well as a difficult means of earning a living. Graves were enclosed in iron cages to frustrate the thieves and the wealthy employed professional guards to watch over the burial plots of their dead. The poor did the job themselves. All protectors were armed and it was not unknown for a grave-robber, while stealing a dead body, suddenly to become a corpse himself.

In spite of all these difficulties, for one surgeon at least, Dr Robert Knox, the problem of providing material for demonstrations was solved by the terrible ingenuity of Burke and Hare.

Robert Knox, who had studied anatomical dissection in London and Paris, returned to Edinburgh in 1822. Four years later he was running the most successful school of anatomy in the city. His great boast which made his school even more popular was: "an ample supply of anatomical subjects." William Burke and William Hare supplied at least sixteen of these subjects to Dr Knox.

William Burke was born in Co Tyrone in 1792. In his youth he joined the Donegal militia and married while stationed in Ballina, Co Mayo. As a result of an argument with his father-in-law over the lease of a small piece of ground, he left his family in 1818 and went to Scotland to work as a navvy on the construction of the Union Canal. While labouring on the diggings, he met Helen (also known as Nelly) McDougal and the two lived afterwards as man and wife.

There is some dispute about William Hare's place of birth but it is generally thought he came from Co Down. Nothing is known of his early life. He also found his way to the Union Canal, where he became friendly with a ganger named Loque, who kept a lodging-house in a narrow alley off the West Port called Tanners Close. When Loque died in 1826, Hare called to console the widow and stayed to take over the premises. Soon afterwards, Nelly McDougal and Burke came to lodge there.

The lodging-house, a filthy hovel, was in a constant state of commotion. No attempt was made to segregate the lodgers, and men, women and occasionally children shared the same quarters. The beds covering the available space—from which all other furniture had been removed—were of sturdy construction and continually occupied by two, three or more guests who paid threepence a night for the privilege. Drink flowed freely and drunken brawls were an everyday event; at night, it seems, those not seriously maimed would engage in sexual orgies. Getting to sleep could not have been easy at Tanners Close. As a contemporary comment suggested: "No surprise could have been excited by cries of murder issuing from such a riotous and disorderly house."

In those squalid lodgings in the West Port, Edinburgh, the murderous career of Burke and Hare started almost by chance, although the first body they sold to a surgeon was not a victim of murder.

One of Hare's lodgers, an old army man who had been ailing for weeks, died on 29 November 1827. Donald, as he was known, had died shortly before he was due to receive his quarterly pension and he owed the Hares four pounds. After discussion of the problem with Burke, Hare decided to recover his loss by selling Donald's corpse to Professor Munro at the university's medical school but, when asked for direction, a student sent them instead to the rooms of his own teacher, Dr Knox, at 10 Surgeon's Square.

That night they received from the doctor's assistants seven pounds ten shillings for the body of the old pensioner and were given an invitation to bring any further material to the same address, where prices as high as £10 could be expected for some specimens. No awkward questions were asked of the sellers.

An opportunity for a second sale presented itself almost immediately when another of Hare's lodgers, a miller called Joseph, was taken ill with a fever. At once, the Hares became alarmed at the prospect of a closure order being placed on the building by the city health authority if the infection were to spread. Urgent action was called for and a frighteningly simple plan was devised after Hare had another conversation with Burke. The partners gave whisky to the already weak patient which enfeebled him further and, while Hare lay across the legs, Burke placed a pillow over the face, keeping it there until the unfortunate man was suffocated. Their method of killing left no signs of violence on the corpse. When the streets were deserted that night, the body was taken in a sack to Surgeon's Square, where Dr Knox's assistants examined it for quality and this time paid the partners £10 for the subject.

The success and simplicity of their joint operation was to be repeated, without a hitch, on more than a dozen occasions over a period of nine months before their terrible secret was discovered. Except for a few characters well known about the city, all their victims were poor, pathetic derelicts without permanent address or family, whose disappearances probably went unnoticed.

Such a woman was Abigail Simpson who was lured to Tanners Close by one or other of the pair on 11 February 1828. The two Irishmen got the old woman drunk—this would become a regular practice—but when it came to the time to kill Abigail, the plan had to be postponed because Burke and Hare were as intoxicated as their visitor. She stayed the night and was murdered the following morning, after having been given more drink, when Burke held her hands and feet, and Hare covered her nose and mouth. Abigail Simpson was frail and struggled very little before she died.

Dr Knox himself was on duty at his lecture rooms when Abigail's remains arrived in a tea-chest. He spoke approvingly of the freshness of the subject, and the two Williams left £10 richer for their troubles. Hare retained £5, Burke's share was £4 and Margaret Hare demanded £1 from this and all other transactions, claiming—with justification—that her premises were the hub of the firm's activities.

In the spring of the year, according to Burke's later confessions, two more murders took place at Tanners Close but, like those of the miller and some others, he could not remember the dates on which they occurred, nor did he know the names of those two victims. But, while he had doubts about dates and the precise order in which they died, Burke had clear recollections of all the murder victims. The first of this unidentified pair was an Englishman who sold matches around the streets of Edinburgh and who, from time to time, lodged with the Hares. While staying at the lodging-house he developed jaundice but his illness was brought to a sudden end by the then familiar method of holding the victim still and suffocating him. The matchseller's death was followed by that of an elderly woman who had been inveigled to the lodging-house by Margaret Hare, with the promise of drink. When the old lady fell asleep Hare, without any assistance from Burke, covered her face with bedclothes and she died in a few moments. Her body, like that of the Englishman before her, was brought to Robert Knox for dissection.

The body of eighteen-year-old Mary Peterson was the next subject taken to Surgeon's Square by Burke and Hare, and—for the first time in their dealings with Knox and his assistants—they were questioned. They were asked to explain how they came in possession of the young girl's remains, as a student at the lecture rooms said he recognised Mary as a prostitute he had been with a few evenings previously, when he had enjoyed the pleasures of her full health and vigour. Burke told his questioners that he had bought the body from an old hag who said Mary had died from drink. This answer was accepted by the easily satisfied surgeons. The real explanation was, of course, different.

On 9 April, Mary Peterson, a strikingly attractive girl, and her friend, Janet Brown, were drinking in a spirit shop in the Canongate when they got into friendly conversation with Burke. Burke's brother, Constantine, lived with his wife at Gibb's Close nearby, and it was to their home that Burke invited his young friends for some dancing and drinking. Con's wife provided the food and then went to inform Hare of the party which was in full swing. Mary Peterson passed out from the effects of rum. She was put in one bed, as Nelly arrived unannounced to hear Burke trying to entice Janet into another. Burke, taking exception to Nelly's abuse and interference, threw a glass at her which opened a wound in her forehead. When he renewed his attentions to Janet, she told him she did not feel she would be of any useful service to him in view of his wife's attitude, and left, promising to return when Nelly was elsewhere. Janet Brown did come back looking for her friend while Burke was out buying more drink, to be told by the Hares and Nelly that Burke and Mary had gone drinking together somewhere in the city.

At that time, Mary Peterson was already dead, having

been murdered by Burke and Hare. And it seems certain that had Burke been there the second time Janet Brown called to the house she would have suffered the same fate as her friend.

Burke's other means of livelihood was shoe-mending. A woman known as Old Effie, who scavenged amongst the city's rubbish for anything useful she could find, knew Burke, calling occasionally to Tanners Close to sell him old boots and leather scraps. On a day in late April she paid a visit to the lodging-house. Burke and Hare murdered her in an adjoining stable after she was first anaesthetised with drink. Like the others, she ended up with the doctors in Surgeon's Square.

Within a few days of Old Effie's suffocation, Burke again displayed the arrogant daring that easy success had fostered in him.

He saw two policemen supporting an old woman. When he asked what it was she had done, he was told she was drunk and was being taken to the West Port police office. Burke replied that he knew the woman, knew where she lived and would be happy to take her home. The officers thanked Burke for his kindness and handed over their burden.

Her corpse was on a dissection-slab later the same day at 10 Surgeon's Square. The doctor's valuation was £10.

There was no slackening of business in June. In the first week of the month, when an Irishwoman, with her twelve-year-old grandson, stopped him to ask directions, Burke knew he had found two more subjects for Dr Knox. After their deaths, which followed the same pattern, Burke and Hare stuffed their bodies into an old fish-barrel and delivered the heavy load to the doctors, who paid £8 for each corpse.

The murder of the young boy, who was a deaf-mute, was to haunt Burke's thoughts until the time of his own death.

As a break from the stress of living in the house in Tanners Close, William Burke and Nelly went on a visit to the home of her family in Stirlingshire. The quartet had not been in close harmony for some time. The incessant bickering of the Hares, which often turned to violence, and the recollection of the murder of the deaf-mute, which he could not shake from his mind, were having a bad effect on Burke's nerves. But the break did nothing to ease the tension at the lodging-house.

On his return to Tanners Close, Burke learned from one of Knox's assistants that in his absence Hare had entered into business on his own account and sold a body to the surgeons for £8. When Burke abused his partner for failing to share the profits, Hare denied the whole transaction. A fierce row developed, resulting in Burke's and Nelly's moving out of the Hares' lodging-house and into the home of John Brogan, whose wife was related to Burke.

Whatever disagreements existed within the gang, or whatever coolness had sprung up between them, Burke and Hare soon realised, even allowing for Hare's solo venture on the market, that unless they operated together they would be ineffective. They settled their differences and it was not long before the pair renewed their partnership, with deadly consequences for other unsuspecting down-and-outs in the city.

They had only resumed operations when Brogan's wife gave birth and, to celebrate the infant's arrival, a party was held at which a Mrs Osler was a guest. Sometime during the festivities she was murdered. Her body was hidden in a coal-cellar and after nightfall was taken the familiar route to Dr Knox, who paid £10 for the subject.

While on the holiday in Stirlingshire, Nelly asked Ann McDougal, her cousin, to visit her in Edinburgh. When the girl accepted the invitation, she was suffocated by Burke and Hare and her corpse netted the top fee.

Hare usually left the preliminary work of procuring victims to Burke, but in the case of Mary Haldine, an elderly prostitute, he made the initial approach himself. Mary knew Hare well and agreed to go with him to his lodging-house to share a bottle of whisky. Like Old Effie before her,

Mary Haldine was murdered in the stable.

When Mary failed to return home her daughter Peggy went searching for her, tracing her mother to Tanners Close. Her enquiries were answered by Hare, who encouraged her to stay for a drink. Peggy agreed, with the inevitable results. In a short time, she appeared on a dissecting-table at Dr Knox's School of Anatomy. Her mother's body was on an adjoining slab. Burke and Hare realised £16 for the pair.

The murderers took a dangerous chance when they picked on their next prey, a distinctive figure, James Wilson. Eighteen-year-old Wilson, an inoffensive simpleton, was a well-known public character who suffered the added affliction of a deformed foot. He supported himself as best he could, usually by begging from the people of Edinburgh, who, even in an age of brutal indifference, generally treated him with kindness and affection. He was certain to be missed. Less certain is the manner in which he was led to his death, as more than one version of the story is recorded. It seems most likely that it was Margaret Hare who brought Daft Jamie, as he was called, to Tanners Close.

In the first week of October 1828 Wilson was led, in Burke's own words, "...as a sheep to the shearer." But in any account of the event there is little dispute as to how he died; Burke held Jamie down while Hare covered the victim's nose and mouth. Because of the youth's great strength, a terrible death struggle took place before he was finally overpowered and taken to Dr Knox. The partners shared £10.

The risk of discovery of the murder of such a popular cripple was considerably lessened by the distinguished anatomist himself. A student who was sure he recognised Jamie was assured by Knox he was mistaken. Knox immediately started the dissection of the corpse.

Burke and Hare's joint enterprise in mass murder could not go for ever undetected, although long immunity from suspicion and interference must have led them to believe that their system of killing for profit was foolproof. No other explanation would seem to account for the unnecessary gamble they took when they murdered their last victim, whose body they casually stored in a house filled with people.

Burke gave a party to celebrate Hallowe'en, inviting to his own lodgings some friends and local residents. Also there to enjoy herself was an Irishwoman, Mrs Doherty, whom Burke had met earlier in the day. After a night of revelry, the partygoers returned to Burke's the following morning. All were there except Mrs Doherty, whose absence was explained away by Nelly, who said their guest had become quarrelsome and had been asked to leave. But Mrs Doherty had not gone anywhere, as a neighbour, Mrs Grey, discovered when she disturbed some straw and found the naked corpse of the Irishwoman. She informed her husband of what she had seen and together they fled the house in search of a policeman.

When the Greys left, Burke and Hare took the body to Robert Knox in a tea-chest, placing it in his cellar for future use. Their reward was £5 there and then, with the promise of a similar amount to be paid later.

In response to the Greys' information, Sergeant-Major John Fisher and patrolman John Finley went to Burke's house to make enquiries. In answer to Fisher, Burke said his visitor had left at seven o'clock in the morning. Nelly's reply to the same query was that the woman had gone away at seven o'clock the night before. Dissatisfied with their contradictory statements, the officers escorted the couple to the police office for further interrogation.

The following morning, on the strength of local rumours that suggested Burke and Hare were resurrectionists—which they were not—Fisher went to 10 Surgeon's Square, where he found a woman's body in the cellar. The Greys and others identified it as that of the late Mrs Doherty. Burke and Nelly claimed to know nothing of the woman's death, and the Hares, when they were brought in for questioning, said they had no idea how Mrs Doherty had died.

Doctors Alexander Black and William Newbigging, and

Robert Christison, professor of medical jurisprudence at Edinburgh University, examined the body. The surgeons agreed that death was not consistent with any known disease but, as no signs of violence appeared on the victim's neck, neither could they explain how breathing had been obstructed, other than by accidental suffocation. *The Courant*, in its issue of 6 November 1828, regretfully announced: "The medical gentlemen who examined the body have not reported, so far as we have heard, that death was occasioned by violence."

The outcome of the post-mortem was a shattering disappointment for the police, and an insurmountable obstacle to the successful prosecution of Burke and Hare and their two women.

The man responsible for bringing the murderers to justice was Sir William Rae, the Lord Advocate. As the four prisoners repeatedly denied any knowledge of the crime and, even more importantly, as the medical evidence was not strong enough to support a charge of murder, he believed the only certain means of securing a conviction was by allowing some of the accused to appear as witnesses against the others. To do otherwise, he felt, was to risk the possibility of all four going free.

An aroused press met this disclosure with predictable rage and the public, appalled to learn of the arrangement, demanded immediate vengeance against the four prisoners.

The statement made by William Hare before the sheriff-substitute on 1 December 1828, implicating his friends in mass killings, was never published. The document mysteriously vanished from the files of the justiciary office. Later, when recalling its contents, Sheriff Duff said it confirmed in substance the sensational revelation of sixteen murders, as admitted in Burke's two confessions made from the condemned cell on 3 and 27 January 1829.

On 8 December Burke and Nelly were officially charged, he with three murders, she with one. Their trial was set for 24 December.

On 23 December the authorities prepared the city of Edinburgh against the threat of mob violence by bringing in three hundred men to augment the regular police force and putting cavalry and infantry units on stand-by. By the early hours of the following morning, thousands of people choked the streets leading to Parliament House, where the High Court of Justiciary sat. The prisoners were already in the building, having been brought there during the night from Calton Jail to frustrate any attempt at public summary justice.

At that court on Christmas Eve, 1828, William Burke and Helen McDougal were tried for murder. Burke was charged with the deaths of Mary Peterson, James Wilson and Mary Doherty. Nelly was charged, on the same indictment, with the murder of Mary Doherty.

The judges who heard the case were Lords Boyle, Meadowbank, Mackenzie and Pitmilly, with Lord Boyle presiding. Sir William Rae led for the Crown. With four counsel allotted to each, the prisoners had the services of eight of Scotland's most eminent lawyers. Sir James Moncrieff took charge of Burke's defence, whilst McDougal's team was headed by Henry Cockburn.

The trial got off to a lively start with Burke's chief counsel questioning the Crown's legal right to charge his client with three murders which, he claimed, were totally unconnected with each other. The judges thought differently but, after much argument, Lord Boyle considered it fairer that Burke should be charged with only one murder. The prosecution chose to proceed with the most recent, that of Mary Doherty. In answer to the charge, both accused pleaded not guilty.

The presentation of evidence began with details of the layout of Burke's lodgings explained by James Briarwood, a builder, who answered a few simple questions and was dismissed. Items of clothing discovered by the police in Burke's rooms were handed to the next witness, Mary Stewart, who identified them as belonging to a former lodger of hers, Mary Doherty. A boarder at the same address, Charles McLaughton, said that when he last saw Mary Doherty on the morning of Friday, 31 October, she appeared to be in the best of health. Important evidence of Burke's meeting with Mrs Doherty and their departure together from a grocery shop was then given by a young assistant, William Noble, who added that he heard Burke inviting the woman back to his lodgings for breakfast.

Memories of the Hallowe'en party and its aftermath were recalled next by several of Burke's neighbours, among them Mrs Grey and her husband. They testified to the finding of the body and of their journey to the police office to report the discovery. Evidence of police reaction to the Greys' information was related by Sergeant-Major Fisher, who told the court how he took Burke and McDougal into custody when answers they gave him aroused his suspicions. He was especially sceptical, he said, of Burke's assertion that the Greys' only reason for reporting a corpse in his room was petty spite, "because he had turned them out for their bad conduct." Fisher's evidence closed with his story of the location and identification of Mrs Doherty's body in Dr Knox's cellar and the subsequent arrest of the prisoners.

So far the evidence before the court contained no surprises, nor was any of the prosecution testimony overturned on cross-examination by the prisoners' counsel. Still the mystery of Mrs Doherty's murder remained; no one yet knew how she had died.

One version of her death was offered to a mesmerised court when the next witness, William Hare, was sworn in at ten o'clock that evening. He was immediately advised about the testimony he would give under oath. Lord Meadowbank promised Hare the certainty of the severest punishment if he lied in his evidence but, on the other hand, if he told the truth, including details of his own part in the killing of the Irishwoman, he was assured that he could "never afterwards be questioned in a court of justice."

Hare told of his early friendship with Burke, described

the Hallowe'en party and explained how Mary Doherty died. During a fight with Burke, when all but Mrs Doherty fled in fright, Hare said he knocked the woman over a stool, quite by accident. When she struck the floor, Burke jumped on her prone body and suffocated her. How did he go about this, the prosecutor wanted to know.

"He put one hand under her nose...and the other under her mouth."

"He stopped her breath, you mean?"

"Yes."

While that frightful scene was taking place, Hare, according to himself, sat by the fire and watched.

When Henry Cockburn asked Hare in cross-examination if he had supplied subjects to the surgeons for dissection apart from the corpse of Mary Doherty, Lord Boyle interjected to remind the witness that he need not answer any questions which might incriminate him: he was not obliged to implicate himself in any way.

Because Hare was under the court's protection, Henry Cockburn had to preface his cross-examination with a warning to the Crown's principal witness that he need not answer any questions concerning his part in the Doherty or other murders.

To most questions, Hare chose not to reply and, when he did give answers, they were couched in an economy of language that made them meaningless. Just the same, Cockburn persisted in cross-examining Hare. His long silences and repeated evasions gave eloquent testimony to his part in the West Port murders as surely as if he had admitted his guilt in open court.

With a baby that cried often in her arms, Margaret Hare was next to testify, after being told by Lord Meadowbank that truthful evidence would guarantee her immunity from prosecution. Like her husband, she was warned of what she could expect if she lied.

Except for the actual murder of Mary Doherty, of which she claimed to know nothing, Margaret's testimony was a rehash of the evidence that was by now completely familiar to everyone. But one answer which she gave to the Lord Advocate brought spectators to the edge of their seats. When asked by Rae what she thought might have happened to Mrs Doherty, Margaret Hare said she supposed she was murdered, and added, without prompting, "I have seen such tricks before." To the then obvious question of why she did not report her suspicions to neighbours or to the authorities, she answered that had she done so she herself would probably have been murdered. Her reply was one of the most revealing statements made at the trial.

The medical experts closed the case for the Crown with evidence that added little of value to its cause.

Dr Alexander Black, who saw the body on 2 November, told the court that the black swollen face suggested to him that Mrs Doherty had died of violence but he would not express an opinion as to the cause of death. Mr Cockburn, in cross-examination, implied that the doctor's description of the body might indicate death by drink. Did the doctor think the appearance of the body was similar to that of a person who had died of intoxication? "Very similar as in this old woman."

Dr Robert Christison, who conducted the post-mortem on the victim on 2 and 3 November, told the Lord Advocate that together with Dr Newbigging he examined the body minutely. He concluded that it was probable the woman had met her death by suffocation but he could not be absolutely certain. He agreed with the prosecutor that she might have died in the manner described by Hare but, when questioned by Cockburn for the defence, he admitted that he had no more than a strong suspicion that the woman had died a violent death. Even when questioned by Lord Boyle, Dr Christison refused to be pinned down to a definite opinion as to how Mary Doherty had died.

When the defence called no witnesses, Sir William Rae made the prosecution's final speech.

He reviewed all aspects of the case, telling the jury that

the bulk of other evidence tended to substantiate the testimony of the Hares. He referred particularly to the undisputed evidence of the obvious good health of Mrs Doherty on the morning of 31 October, to her meeting with Burke, sworn to by the shop assistant, to her presence at the Hallowe'en gathering where she was seen by several witnesses to enjoy herself and to the discovery of her corpse in Burke's lodgings on 1 November by Mrs Grey. All this evidence, together with the police testimony, the prosecutor said, must lead any sensible person to the only conclusion possible—that the two prisoners were guilty as charged. Understandably, the Lord Advocate did not dwell on the medical findings. Almost as an afterthought, he finished by saying that by her lies McDougal had tried to conceal the murder and was therefore as guilty as Burke.

Sir James Moncrieff and Mr Henry Cockburn, for the accused couple, pointed out the glaring weaknesses of the Crown's case. Both counsel instructed the jurors to eliminate from their minds all of the Hares' evidence as being unworthy of belief. Speaking on behalf of Burke, Sir James told the jury that the Hares would say anything to save their own necks. And, without the Hares' stories, what had the prosecution proved? Nothing. Or, at best, that a body had been sold to Robert Knox for dissection—but that was a long way from murder, the crime for which his client stood charged. As for the medical evidence, Moncrieff said it must be discounted. Mrs Doherty might have died by accident, natural causes, wilful murder, or the effects of drink. He could not be sure nor, he claimed, could anyone else, and that included the medical experts. And, in the absence of any clear picture of how the woman died, defence counsel warned the jury that it would be dangerous to assume Burke's guilt simply because he seemed the most probable culprit. Finally, he declared that no one would ever again be safe in Scotland if a man's life could be ended on the evidence of such a villain as Hare. He invited the jury to bring in a verdict of not guilty.

In opening his plea for Helen McDougal, Henry Cockburn said his client was not involved in the violence used against the victim. However the woman died, McDougal had played no part in her death, having left the room with Mrs Hare and others when alarmed at the brawling of Burke and Hare. If she was an accessory after the fact, as claimed by the Crown, it was due to her refusal to betray Burke, whom she looked upon as her husband, and her efforts to conceal his suspected guilt were understandable. The very worst that could be said against her was that she had failed to disclose knowledge of a crime. Ending his speech, Cockburn advised the jury, if they could not be certain of her direct involvement in the death of Mary Doherty, to find the case against Helen McDougal not proven.

The last hours of the trial were given over to Lord Boyle's summing-up, followed by the jury's deliberations.

The presiding judge said that, while the defence lawyers advised them to discount the evidence of the Hares, he thought it would be unwise of the jury to do so. While he and his fellow judges believed the witnesses might have been involved in other crimes, he stressed that in this particular case he thought their stories were credible. Although he advised the jury to give the benefit of any doubt to the prisoners, the judge made it clear where his own feelings lay. His charge to the jurors was heavily weighed against Burke and McDougal.

The jury's consideration of the case lasted a scant fifty minutes. As expected, they found Burke guilty of murder. He was sentenced to be hanged on 28 January 1829. The case against Helen McDougal was not proven and she was freed, perhaps reflecting the jury's belief that to hang Nelly while Hare was given the Crown's protection would have been a scandalous abuse of justice.

At ten o'clock on Christmas morning the court rose, having sat without interruption for twenty-four hours.

During much of that time, the audience had listened in fascinated horror to the chilling story of a merciless criminal industry. Yet in the eerie gloom of Parliament Hall only one of the quartet responsible stood convicted and public bitterness increased with the news of Nelly's release.

The three who evaded punishment experienced social ostracism, as did Robert Knox, whom many believed should have stood in the dock with the accused.

Helen McDougal, after two dangerous encounters with hostile crowds, returned to her home in Stirlingshire, only to find she was as despised there as she had been in Edinburgh. There is a report of her having been seen in Newcastle in January 1829 but after that she vanishes.

Margaret Hare was similarly abused by vengeful mobs and rescued by the police and jailed for her own protection. The *Evening Courant* of 14 February reports on an enormous crowd that had gathered outside the Calton police office in the hope of seeing the departure of Hare's wife to Greenock. From there, the authorities had arranged her passage to Belfast in the *Fingal* on 12 February. There is nothing more known of Margaret Hare.

The trail of William Hare, who left Edinburgh on 5 February, disappears after his arrival in Carlisle. While travelling south, he was recognised in Dumfries where a threatening crowd jammed the High Street, forcing him to take refuge in the King's Arms. He was escorted from the town with police protection and was last reported seen outside Carlisle by a mailcoach driver who knew him.

Oppressed by thoughts of Hare's freedom, Burke lapsed into despair in his condemned cell. On 3 January he made a full confession to the authorities, which seemed to ease his tormented mind. A second statement, made on the twenty-seventh of the month to a newspaper reporter, varied only slightly from the original.

On the morning of his execution, more than 20 000 people thronged the approaches to the scaffold. A great roar greeted the condemned man, who prayed for a few moments while the hangman prepared him for the drop. At the agreed signal of a dropped handkerchief, the executioner released the trap and William Burke was dead.

Like that of his unfortunate victims, Burke's body ended up on an anatomist's slab; it was publicly dissected by Professor Munro. To avert a riot, Munro's colleague, Professor Christison, arranged for a public viewing of the corpse. An estimated 30 000 passed Burke's partly dissected body, an impressive lying-in-state. Burke's skeleton was preserved and can be seen today in the Anatomy Museum of Edinburgh University.

2

DEATH OF A JOURNALIST

Daniel McFarland   New York, 1870

In the winter of 1869 the Reverend Henry Ward Beecher was
at the height of his career. As pastor of fashionable Plymouth
congregationalist church in Brooklyn, New York, he
ministered to more than two thousand worshippers, the
largest congregation in America. Best known for his stand
against slavery, he was also famous for unorthodox
theological opinions and for holding a sentimental view of
women. But even for Beecher, who led one of the most
eccentric lives in nineteenth-century America, the marriage
ceremony he performed in a New York hotel bedroom on 30
November 1869 was a bizarre and newsworthy event. The
groom, noted journalist and author, Albert D Richardson,
who lay dying in bed from a bullet wound, was married to
Abby McFarland, a woman who, it would later be claimed,
already had a husband. Aided by two fellow clergymen, the
Reverend Beecher prayed for the couple, speaking glowingly
of the joys of the next world and understandably saying
little of this one, from which the unfortunate Richardson
departed two days later. Within hours the marriage was the
talk of New York; the next day it was the talk of America.
Daniel McFarland, Abby's previous husband, had been
lodged in the notorious city jail, known then and now as
The Tombs, to await trial for attempting to kill Richardson

in the office of the *New York Tribune* on 25 November. After Richardson's death, McFarland languished in jail until April of the following year, when he was charged with the murder of the journalist. It was said at the time that he could have been released had he applied for bail but on the advice of his lawyers he had refrained from doing so, hoping to gain sympathy as a wronged and persecuted husband.

The sensation created by the shooting of Richardson and his strange marriage and death, lasted right through to spring. The involvement of a large number of prominent citizens and notable eccentrics added extra spice to the drama. Even more than his murder, Richardson's deathbed wedding provided endless material for editorials in newspapers nationwide. With the case being given whole pages in the newspapers and national and world news often dismissed with a few lines, many of the facts surrounding the murder case were brought to the public's attention long before McFarland was brought to trial.

He was born in Ireland in 1819 and emigrated with family to America while still a youth. At his trial, James McFarland, his elder brother, gave information about their boyhood but managed to do so without mentioning the location of their home in Ireland, and Abby McFarland, in a sworn statement concerning her life with her husband, merely said McFarland was an Irishman.

The family lived for a short time in Brooklyn, before settling in Patterson, New Jersey. Within four years of their arrival both parents had died and the older brothers, James and Owen, had moved to Philadelphia, leaving Daniel to fend for himself. He proved to be a resourceful and energetic youth. Working first as a machinist and later as a harness-maker, he managed to save enough to enable him to study, eventually graduating with a degree in arts from Dartmouth College. He later went to Paris, where he studied law. It is known that he broke his journey to visit some Irish relations on his way back to America. On his return to his adopted country in 1851 McFarland was admitted to the

Massachusetts Bar.

Daniel McFarland practised as a lawyer for less than a year, preferring to devote his talents to business—mostly dealing in land—at which he became a success. While on a visit to Manchester, New Hampshire, to view some property, he met Abby Sage, of whom a defence lawyer would later say, "She was a poor factory-girl at the time, without education..." They were married in Boston in December 1857. She was nineteen, he thirty-six.

Misfortune overtook the pair early in the marriage when their first child, a daughter, Jessie, died soon after birth. In her statement sworn on 9 May 1870, soon after the conclusion of her husband's trial, Mrs McFarland said the baby's death seemed to affect McFarland greatly. When not rude and dismissive towards her, he became moody and depressed, often remaining silent for days at a time. About this period, he started to drink heavily, sometimes threatening Abby with violence. Although they would later produce two sons, both born at Abby's parents' home, McFarland and his wife lived as often apart as together, she claiming that drink had come to dominate his life. Neglect of his affairs along with careless speculation during the years of the civil war resulted in the complete collapse of his property business, which sowed the seeds of further despondency. Charles Spencer, one of McFarland's attorneys, told at a later date what next happened to his client: "He became a commissioner of enrolment and afterwards worked for the Provost Marshal and subsequently became connected with the collection of internal revenues of the country."

As a tax assessor, McFarland's work took him to many business premises, including the office of the *New York Tribune*. There he met and became friends with Albert D Richardson, returned war correspondent, something of a hero and a shareholder in that newspaper.

Abby McFarland also knew Richardson, having first met him in 1866 at the home of the *Tribune* publisher, Samuel Sinclair. At this time of changing society, the Sinclairs' home, at 8 Washington Place, was considered the centre of liberal thought, where the conflict between the old respectability and the new morality was constantly being discussed. Newspapers hostile to the *Tribune* saw Sinclair and his friends as radical intellectuals and philosophers striving to loosen the bonds of social convention, while living lives of unrestrained passion and advocating liberalism and free love. The women reformers of the group came in for the severest criticism. They were portrayed as a radical coterie, whose advanced notions about female emancipation and easier divorce laws were described as a disgrace to decency and an insult to the women of America. But critical reaction was mixed. A substantial body of American opinion favoured a more liberal approach to life after the upheavals of the civil war. The *Tribune* championed the new liberalism but, unlike his wife, McFarland was never a part of the bohemian bustle at Washington Place. Nevertheless, from associations formed during his years of prosperity, he had many powerful friends in commerce, industry and the legal profession. These men would later come to his aid, causing a wide rift in Sinclair's group which mirrored the division of opinion across America.

At Sinclair's literary gatherings, Abby McFarland made friends with Mrs Lucia Calhoun, a writer of children's stories and a leading light in the emerging feminist movement. Prompted by her new friend to express herself artistically, Mrs McFarland gave poetry readings at New York's Steinway Hall, where she was warmly received by her audience. With Mrs Calhoun's encouragement and Richardson's practical help, she then took to the professional stage, seeking perhaps the attention and approval she no longer received at home. Largely on Richardson's recommendation, Mrs McFarland was given her first acting role on 20 November 1866 by Edwin Booth, famed actor and owner of New York's Winter Garden Theatre.

From then onwards, McFarland's self-control seemed to desert him as his drinking bouts became more frequent. He was soon attracting great attention to himself as he roamed New York constantly complaining to anyone who would listen to him of his strong objections to his wife identifying herself with people of the theatre. He also made it known that he thoroughly disapproved of her literary friends and their ideas. His domestic troubles, already widely suspected, became common knowledge with his irrational behaviour, and no doubts were left when his wife confided to Mrs Calhoun and others that she was seriously thinking of leaving her husband, whom, she said, she now feared. Gradually, as she came more and more under the dominating influence of Albert Richardson, her relationship with McFarland worsened. On 21 February 1867, she left her home at 72 Amity Street with her son Percy: "I went to Mr Sinclair's house and placed myself under the protection of his roof and never afterwards saw Mr McFarland, except once or twice in the presence of others." Despite the collective efforts of their friends to restore her to her husband, Abby was adamant she would never return to McFarland. She would, she said, divorce him if this were possible. Whatever about the fear of her husband and his aggressive and occasionally violent conduct, it is probable that her final parting from him took place on the advice of the Sinclairs, who had urged her several times earlier to remove her son Percy from McFarland's control. The younger boy, Danny, was already living with her parents in New Hampshire.

With both partners trying to impose versions of the truth upon their friends—often the same people—it soon became clear that, even given a period of separation and reflection, there was little possibility of the warring McFarlands settling their differences. This belief was confirmed within weeks, when Daniel McFarland moved to new accommodation and Abby McFarland returned with Percy to her former lodgings in Amity Street. Richardson moved there soon after. It is certain that Richardson's assurances that he and Abby occupied separate quarters did nothing to alleviate McFarland's inner tension. Living alone probably heightened his sense of loneliness and gloom but it was a visit to the *Tribune* building on 11 March that triggered his next decisive action. McFarland was given a letter to pass on to his wife by Elisha Sinclair, the publisher's brother. He could have shown better judgement. Although it was addressed to his wife, McFarland opened it and found it was a gushing love letter, written by Richardson to Abby, expressing his most intimate sentiments. Two days later, Daniel McFarland shot Albert Richardson.

As the journalist was escorting Mrs McFarland along Thomas Street after she had finished a performance at the Waverley Theatre, her enraged husband fired three shots at Richardson's back from a distance of about six feet. It is probable McFarland was drunk. Two of the bullets missed their target completely and the third had such little effect on Richardson that he was able to grab and hold on to his attacker until the police arrived. His injuries were slight but his immediate recovery only postponed the inevitable; it did not prevent it. A major tragedy was in the making.

McFarland cannot have hoped to get away with his murderous attack but he did. No charges were pressed by Richardson, who said he wished to shield Mrs McFarland from further anguish and embarrassment. There were those who would take a less charitable view of the journalist's refusal to pursue McFarland through the courts. At Daniel McFarland's trial for murder, three years later, his attorneys introduced into the evidence the records of the Jefferson Market police court for 14 March 1867, which showed that McFarland had been released without charge. This fact, the defence lawyers claimed, clearly indicated that Richardson understood the reason for, and fully appreciated the justice of, McFarland's armed attack upon him.

Within a few weeks of the shooting, Daniel McFarland was again involved in legal matters. At the end of March, he started proceedings to get possession of his eldest child. In November of the same year, despite the apparent unstable mental state of McFarland, Percy was handed over to his father. This decision caused Abby McFarland great distress as her husband refused her access to the boy even when she called accompanied by mutual friends. In the spring of 1868, hoping to bring legal pressure to bear, she arrived at McFarland's lodgings with her lawyer, asking to see Percy. She was met by her husband "with such a storm of outrage and abuse as I will not try to describe." Mrs McFarland unburdened herself to many of her friends, who, in turn, offered their advice. There was no doubt in Mrs Calhoun's mind what this advice should be—Abby must get a divorce.

Mrs McFarland went to live in the state of Indiana and stayed for more than a year. She needed a residence qualification to be granted some form of legal separation from her husband. Many maintained it had no standing in law outside the limits of the small town in which it had taken place. This is how Charles Spencer, one of McFarland's counsel, would describe it to the jury: "We have heard a rumour—in a small obscure town in a remote county in that paradise for adulterers, Indiana—some kind of mockery was performed. An infamy to legislation and a libel to civilisation." Nowhere in the trial record is Abby's status clearly defined; depending on counsel, she was either McFarland's wife or Richardson's widow. This is just one argument that resulted from the uncertainty of her exact legal relationship with the victim and the accused. Abby's mother, Mrs Sage, was asked by John Davis, for the State: "You are the mother of Mrs Richardson, formerly Mrs McFarland, are you not?"

"I am."

Mr Graham, for the defence, interrupted before Davis could ask any further questions of Mrs Sage: "If your Honour please, we must positively object to questions being put in that form. It has not yet appeared that the woman who was Mrs McFarland has ever ceased to be Mrs McFarland and we shall object to this form of question."

But John Graham got little satisfaction from Judge Hackett, who simply said that the witness had already answered the question. Yet the mix-up continued; each time Abby's name was mentioned, a three-cornered dogfight would erupt to amuse the spectators and confuse the jury.

Mrs McFarland returned from Indiana to her parents' home on 31 October 1869. On 17 November, Albert Richardson called to discuss their marriage plans but nothing definite had been agreed before Richardson had to go back to New York.

While his wife had been living in Indiana, McFarland was following his familiar routine of telling the story of his misfortunes to any ready listener, often weeping as he did so. With his moods shifting between drunken self-pity and unreasonable optimism, he had become a nuisance to even his closest friends, though, to their credit, they mostly stood by him. Adding to his troubles and the concern of his colleagues was his heavy dependence on drugs, which, he said, he now urgently needed to help him sleep and work.

McFarland first learned of his wife's divorce on 23 November 1869. His condition then was described by a lawyer friend who met him on that day as "disordered," though this could have been induced by drink or drugs. He seems to have brooded for two days before walking into the *Tribune* building just after 5.00p.m. on the twenty-fifth. There he asked to speak to Richardson. When told the newspaperman was absent, he sat down in the accounts office, saying he would wait. Albert Richardson appeared about 5.30. McFarland rose from his chair, moved towards the new arrival and, without speaking a single word, shot Richardson in the stomach in front of six witnesses. He then left the *Tribune* building and walked casually to the Westmoreland Hotel at the corner of 17th Street and 4th Avenue. In his own name, he booked into the hotel and remained there drinking, as though nothing had happened, until he was traced and arrested by Captain Anthony Allaine at 10.00p.m. that night. He was charged with attempted murder.

After the shooting Albert Richardson was taken to the

nearby Astor House, where he was attended by the hotel's resident physician, Dr Charles Swan. There was nothing the doctor could do for his dangerously sick patient, except ease the suffering with regular administrations of morphine. He lingered for a week and when he became aware that his death was very near at hand, Richardson asked that he be married to Abby McFarland. It was a tall order but, with the help of the ever-romantic Mrs Calhoun, the wedding was arranged. She contacted the Rev Beecher, who conducted the ceremony with a good deal of improvisation and the aid of two equally inventive assistants. Albert Richardson died on 2 December. He was thirty-six years old.

The debate about McFarland's guilt or innocence raged furiously as the trial date approached. The public were divided. For those who regarded him as a victim, as many more considered him a callous killer.

Every major newspaper in America was represented in court, with some newspaper owners, it was said, sending as many as six special correspondents to provide daily accounts of the case for a thoroughly roused nation.

Daniel McFarland's trial for first-degree murder opened on 4 April 1870 at the Court of General Sessions, New York. Judge Hackett, recorder of New York, presided. The case for the People was presented by New York District Attorney, John Garvin, with John Davis as co-prosecutor. For the defence McFarland's friends provided him with a trio of eminent lawyers, John Graham, Elbridge Gerry and Charles Spencer. Three full days were needed to choose a jury acceptable to both sides and the trial proper did not start until the morning of 7 April.

George King, a young man who worked for the *Tribune*, was the first witness called by the prosecution. To a series of questions put to him by District Attorney Garvin, King told the jury of seeing McFarland shoot Richardson in the counting-room of the newspaper. Garvin summarised: "Now, if I understand you, the prisoner stood on the inside of the counter, Richardson came up on the outside of the counter, enquired for his letters; the prisoner leaned over, reached across you and fired?"

"Yes sir."

Mr Graham jumped to his feet, shouting at the district attorney: "Don't sum up. You have understood the evidence if you kept your ears open."

"I don't know you heard it," Garvin answered.

"We will take care of ourselves," snapped Graham.

The hearing was scarcely twenty minutes old when this heated exchange occurred, and it set the tone for what was to follow as opposing counsel tried to outdo each other in torrents of mutual recriminations. The distinction between abuse and reasonable dissent never became clear during the whole length of the trial. With each recurring clash the protagonists became more entrenched and belligerent, and the result was that it was often difficult for witnesses to hear or be heard. The trial, which lasted twenty-six days and divided the American people into two rival camps, was conducted in such an atmosphere of intermittent uproar as to be almost beyond the control of Recorder Hackett.

After five of King's colleagues from the newspaper's accounts department had corroborated his story, Captain Allaine of the 4th Precinct gave evidence of arresting the prisoner at the Westmoreland Hotel. In cross-examination, the officer was severely criticised by Mr Graham, over the persistent objections of the district attorney, for taking the accused to the Astor House where Richardson identified McFarland as his attacker. The defence claimed that the prisoner's rights had been infringed when he had not been taken directly to the police station and formally charged. In any case, Richardson had not been in a fit state to make a positive identification.

A further related controversy erupted some time later, when Dr Swan was being cross-examined by the defence. Earlier, for the district attorney, the doctor had described the course of the bullet. It had entered the epigastric region, passed along the liver, into the stomach and out again where it next penetrated the intestines and finally came to lodge beneath the skin in the left lumbar region of the back. There were massive injuries caused by the bullet, and these injuries, said Dr Swan, had brought about the death of the victim. McFarland's lawyer skirted round the witness's evidence of the gunshot wound, and drew from the doctor that several doses of morphine had been administered to Richardson to ease his pain. With this information on record, Graham asked Judge Hackett to dismiss the case against his client, contending that Albert Richardson could just as easily have died from narcotic poisoning as from a bullet wound. With the dismissal of this motion by Recorder Hackett, District Attorney Garvin, after first accusing Graham of theatrical posturing and insulting the intelligence of the jury, told the court he had no further evidence to present.

Convinced of the seemingly obvious strength of his case, Garvin had called only a handful of witnesses. The prosecutor believed the evidence of the arresting officer together with that of those who had seen the actual shooting and the medical testimony of Dr Swan were all that was needed to bring a quick conclusion to the trial. So clear-cut did it all seem to him, that it took just a single day for the district attorney to present his case to the jury. But he was very much astray in his judgement. The trial would run for another twenty-two days, during which time spectators would tell their absent friends it was the best entertainment in New York.

Charles Spencer began his efforts to save the life of the accused by attacking the character of the victim but quickly changed direction after a hurried consultation with his associate counsel. Elbridge Gerry and John Graham, realising how popular Richardson had been with the public, warned Spencer against excessive criticism of the dead journalist, though before the trial would end they too would attack the good name of several honest citizens. It was the first disagreement among McFarland's attorneys, and there would be others.

When he resumed, Spencer for a while tempered his address to the jury. He said that at the time of his wedding, Albert Richardson was so mentally incapacitated by the administration of drugs that he was incapable of appreciating the moral consequences of the event. In other words, he said, Richardson was put in a position where he did not know what he was doing. And Spencer made no bones about whom he was holding responsible for having arranged the blasphemous ceremony, the excitement of which, he contended, had contributed to the death of the victim. Ignoring the loud objections of both prosecuting attorneys, Charles Spencer named Mrs Calhoun as chief intriguer in the love affair of Abby McFarland and Albert Richardson. But when the defendant's lawyer described the well-known feminist as "a plotter, a conspirator, adventurer and procuress, from beginning to end," there was an explosion of noise from all sides of the courtroom. As opposing counsel roared insults at each other, spectators clapped and cheered like children at a circus, while Recorder Hackett threatened to jail all five lawyers for gross contempt of court. When order was eventually restored to the proceedings, the judge rebuked the onlookers for their unruly behaviour which, he said, was almost as disgusting as that of the lawyers. Any recurrence, he warned, would result in a clearance of the courtroom. He never acted upon his threat though he often had cause to do so, for as the trial went on attacks on the character of witnesses became more and more vicious, resulting in further noisy outbursts from the spectators.

Charles Spencer's much-interrupted opening address got back on course with a reluctantly advanced third factor being introduced as an explanation for Richardson's death. Defence counsel informed the jury that, if the victim had not died of an overdose of poison given him by Dr Swan, or if he had not died of over-excitement occasioned by his pagan wedding, then he may have died of a bullet fired by his client. If this were the case, and he was not for a moment admitting the fact, then Daniel McFarland was insane at the time he pulled the trigger. This is how the lawyer explained McFarland's actions: "...a sensitive mind laid in ruins by wrongs accumulated upon him by a wife-seducer and child-robber sent to eternity by the hand of a husband and father, wronged, in a moment when the angry waves of a great sea overwhelmed him, turning away his reason." McFarland was portrayed as a man overtaken by sadness and misfortune whose condition rapidly deteriorated with an excessive intake of alcohol and strong medicines until eventually his mind became unsettled. The jury would surely understand the state of McFarland's mind at the time of the shooting, Spencer suggested, and he knew that he could trust them to bring in a verdict of Not Guilty.

After his appeal for the jury's sympathetic consideration of his client's mental condition, Spencer abandoned all pretence at a rational presentation of the facts. His address relapsed into a tirade of abuse directed again at Mrs Calhoun and at the *Tribune*, its staff and its publisher. Nor did Sinclair's own family and friends escape the lawyer's acid tongue. Even by the standards of American courtroom practice—not renowned for restraint—Spencer had gone too far in blackening the good name of innocent people, many of whom were staunch supporters of his client, a fact the lawyer unaccountably ignored.

The following morning, after a brief consultation with Judge Hackett, Charles Spencer made an apology in open court, asking that his remarks about Mrs Calhoun and others be seen as over-zealous rather than vindictive and caused by his deep concern for the plight of Daniel McFarland. He was then completely bewildered by the unexpectedness of the reception he received when he returned to his colleagues behind the defence table. Graham and Gerry were so antagonised by what they saw as Spencer's weakness that the three of them almost came to blows. As the judge tried to control the disorder, Spencer took to his heels and was not seen again for the remainder of the trial.

His absence was hardly noticed, for attorneys Graham and Gerry continued in similar abusive fashion until the trial's end. Highly diverting and entertaining though these antics were, they could only sustain the interest of spectators and the reading public for so long. After a week or so, an air of humdrum routine had overtaken the case, and there were reports of people falling asleep in court—some of them jurors.

The defence lawyers produced several doctors who testified to having prescribed large doses of various powerful medicines including morphine, Indian hemp, and bromide of potassium for McFarland. According to these medical witnesses their patient had suffered involuntary twitching of the facial muscles and flashes of light and dark specks before his eyes, the pupils of which had contracted; and he had delusions and hallucinations, with doubts, at times, as to his own identity. Some of the force of this evidence was offset by the testimony of two doctors called in rebuttal by the district attorney. They said there was nothing wrong with McFarland. And a number of other witnesses for the prosecution swore that they had known McFarland and not heard him say or notice him do anything which suggested to them he was mentally ill.

The bickering continued with each point bitterly contested by opposing counsel as the trial dragged on to its final days. Then on Tuesday 3 May a new excitement was generated for a while by the entry of Mrs Lucia Calhoun—recently remarried and now Mrs Runkle—who became the object of intense curiosity. She did not appear to be the scheming ogre the spectators had been led to expect. A slim woman of less than thirty, she was elegantly dressed in black silk and spoke in a quiet but firm voice, giving decisive answers to all of Graham's questions.

She denied being involved in an intrigue and would not admit that any intrigue had existed. She was, she said, a friend who had tried to help Abby McFarland overcome the cruelties of her husband. Bullying tactics by McFarland's lawyer could not get her to alter her evidence which was a reiteration of her testimony given to John Davis in direct examination. Before releasing the witness, John Graham insinuated that Mrs Runkle and others had conspired to influence the outcome of the trial by providing funds to pay Davis to assist the district attorney in prosecuting the case. In a series of questions he also suggested that there had been tampering with witnesses:

"Mrs Runkle, have you or your husband disbursed any money for the purposes of this prosecution?"

"I never have, to my knowledge."

"Have you been directly or indirectly engaged in procuring counsel for this prosecution?"

"I have not."

"Has your husband, to your knowledge?"

"Not to my knowledge."

"Have you seen any witnesses for the purpose of supplying testimony?"

"No one."

"Has he?"

"Not to my knowledge."

A little later, in an obvious attempt to connect the witness with the Sinclair camp, defence counsel asked this question, and was probably surprised by the answer:

"Your father is employed in the *Tribune* office?"

"No sir, he never was."

After answering some further questions on McFarland's attitude towards his wife's acting ambitions, Mrs Runkle was dismissed and, with her exit from the scene, the trial was at a virtual end.

John Graham took two days to make the closing speech for the defence, which he peppered with biblical and Latin quotations, with arguments drawn from history, poetry, Shakespeare and the common law of England, citing judgements that were centuries old. It must have been an exhausting experience for the jury who, unlike the spectators, could not by choice escape the courtroom.

The basis of Graham's plea was temporary insanity. Denouncing Abby McFarland's alliance with Richardson as totally corrupt, he said that McFarland's ordinary senses had been disordered by "the unholy, reckless and lawless passion of a bold and bad libertine." He was not to be held responsible for what he did but exonerated from the results of his act because his mind was disturbed by provocation. In fact, said his lawyer, men like McFarland who tried to protect and uphold the purity of American womanhood deserved the law's protection, not its punishment.

Nearing the end of his address, McFarland's counsel reminded the jury of its responsibilities. "Meet them like husbands, fathers, men. The highest interests of society are involved in these proceedings...the desecration of the marriage relation creates as no other emotion in a manly bosom that of mere manly passion for revenge!" In other words, McFarland did only what might be expected of any red-blooded American placed in a similar position.

Closing for the State, District Attorney Garvin dismissed Graham's argument as hogwash. He attacked McFarland's lawyers for their conduct of the case, saying they had hampered the course of justice by what amounted to an approval of Albert Richardson's murder by the accused. As far as McFarland himself was concerned, his supposed insanity was nothing more than a fraud. Previously he had attempted to kill Richardson and his failure to kill the journalist had only aggravated McFarland's hatred of him. The second attempt had succeeded and now Daniel McFarland must pay the penalty by forfeiting his own life. Garvin appealed to the jury not to be swayed by emotion; they must be firm in their resolution, he told them, and convict the prisoner as the evidence demanded.

At two o'clock on the last day of the trial, Recorder Hackett began his charge to the jury with a remark that could have been faulted by few: "Gentlemen of the jury, to you and all others who have assisted in this trial, it must be an especial cause of congratulation that it rapidly draws to a close." He then cautioned them that they could neither convict nor acquit the prisoner on the strength of the behaviour or the power of the speeches of counsel. Only evidence, which he knew they would carefully consider, should be entertained in assessing the innocence or guilt of the accused. Rumour and gossip were to have no place in their deliberations. Although the judge stressed that a wronged husband could not take the law into his own hands, it was generally considered that Recorder Hackett's summing-up had favoured McFarland.

After an hour and fifty-five minutes, the jury returned with a verdict of Not Guilty, the second word of their decision drowned in a sudden roar of sound. One report described the reaction to the verdict as being "one long clear sound that seemed to proceed from one throat. It shook the windows and seemed to vibrate back from the very walls."

Elsewhere the verdict was greeted with less enthusiasm. Cynics of the time had no difficulty in believing that the money and influence of powerful friends had bought McFarland his freedom. How they could have done so was never specified, though reports then circulating suggested that these friends, who had set themselves up as custodians of the private morals of the community, had exerted pressure on some members of the jury and had even induced defence lawyers to conduct their case in a particular manner. No such conspiracy was discovered, probably because none had ever existed, though a question remained concerning the cost of McFarland's defence, which was enormous.

But more than the verdict, the public's greatest criticism was levelled at the lawyers. Of those engaged in the case, none displayed the professional discipline expected of such eminent men and none emerged with credit from a trial that seemed as indifferent to facts as it did to moderate language or ordinary manners. And Recorder Hackett earned no laurels either for his handling of the case. Because of his fragile grip on the trial, established court procedure and conduct was only loosely observed, sometimes not at all.

His least excusable fault was his continuous failure to protect witnesses from the gratuitous insults hurled at them by counsel on both sides of the courtroom.

But little had changed after the public clamour had died down. Many thought a just decision had been reached by the jury, while masses of Americans saw Daniel McFarland's acquittal as a scandalous miscarriage of justice.

3

THE BARNES MYSTERY

Kate Webster   London, 1879

On Tuesday, 8 July 1879, at the Central Criminal Court, Old Bailey, London, Mr Justice Denman said to Kate Webster just before the end of her trial for murder: "Whether your statement now be true or not, God only can tell." He was referring to her latest story in which she accused an unnamed man of being the real murderer. But the judge's observation might have applied to almost every statement Kate uttered, and one difficulty in attempting to unearth the facts about any incident in her life is that she seemed incapable of telling the truth about anything. Although she was recognised at the time of her trial as an obsessive liar, it was the fury of her attack upon her victim and her method of disposing of the body afterwards that earned Kate Webster everlasting infamy.

She was born Catherine Lawlor in Enniscorthy, Co Wexford, in 1849 as Ireland struggled to overcome the ravages of the potato famine. She was to give several versions of her early life, one of which was colourful enough to include marriage to a ship's captain and the birth of four children, all of whom were supposed to have died in infancy. But nothing is really known about her until she went to England where, except for a two-year gap, her life is fairly well documented. She was first arrested in 1867 on a charge of larceny. On conviction she was sentenced to four years' imprisonment in the city of Liverpool.

Moving south after being released, she spent the next couple of years, according to herself, living an honest life working as a domestic servant in different locations in and about London. In view of her criminal history, this does not seem very likely but there is no accurate record of what she was doing at this time and contemporary accounts differ. What is known is that in 1874 she was living at 5 Acre Road, Kingston, and at that address on 19 April she gave birth to a son. The father of the child then deserted her. "I had to thieve for that child and go to prison for it," as she later described her predicament in court.

In the matter of her name, Kate was fairly flexible. At different times and places she referred to herself as Webb, Shannon, Lawlor—her proper name—and Lawless, surely the most fitting. It was about this time that she took to calling herself Mrs Webster and managed a meagre and precarious living by swindling local shopkeepers and robbing lodging-houses of small items which she then sold to pawnbrokers and dealers in second-hand goods.

So that she might continue these activities and at the same time avoid arrest, frequent changes of address were necessary. But even so, her career of petty crime was so frantic at this period that it was only a matter of time before she was taken into custody. She had been eventually traced to Teddington where, on 4 May 1875, she faced a total of thirty-six charges including larceny and false pretences. She was convicted on all counts and sentenced to eighteen months' hard labour, which she served in Wandsworth Prison. When given her liberty Kate continued to move from place to place and, predictably having learned nothing from her latest experience of jail, was soon again in trouble with the authorities. She was to serve two further short terms of imprisonment before moving on 13 January 1879 to 3 Mitchell Road, Richmond, the house of Mrs Sarah Crease, a friend of hers who had been taking care of her son.

On a day during Kate's stay at Mitchell Road, Mrs Crease took ill and was unable to do her regular job of cleaning for a Miss Lucy Loader who lived nearby. Kate went in Sarah's place. So impressed was the mistress of the house with Kate's industry and willingness to please that she advised her to go along to 2 Vine Cottages, Park Road, Richmond, and see a friend of hers, Mrs Julia Thomas, who was then looking for a general maid. Whether or not it was her intention, Kate later claimed she was genuinely seeking a job in domestic service. Just as easily, of course, she may have seen it as an opportunity to steal valuables which she could sell to dealers, as she had previously done, but whatever her motive, she acted on Miss Loader's suggestion and went to talk to Mrs Thomas. If Kate is to be believed, Julia Thomas dispensed with all formality and asked for no references, saying simply that Miss Loader's recommendation was good enough. Almost immediately it was agreed that Kate should take up her duties as housekeeper on 27 January 1879.

Mrs Julia Thomas, a retired school teacher, was twice widowed. From the time she buried her second husband in 1873, until she moved to Richmond in 1878, she had lived alone. There was, apart from the obvious differences, a curious similarity between Julia Thomas and Kate Webster. Both mistress and maid seemed to lack any element of permanence in their lives. Kate, of course, had her own reasons for shifting. Mrs Thomas also could not settle for any length of time at an address before her restlessness impelled her to move on. She did this frequently, worrying her relations who, on one occasion at least, had to seek police assistance in locating her.

She had taken up residence at 2 Vine Cottages the previous September when she leased the cottage from the owner, Miss Elizabeth Ives, who, with her mother Mrs Jane Ives, lived in the adjoining property. In those four months, Julia Thomas became a familiar figure in the neighbourhood. She was well known as something of an oddity with a passion for parade and show, as she dressed in flamboyant clothes adorned with an excess of jewellery. But, although she was well known, Mrs Thomas was not unanimously well liked. Because of her unpredictable temperament servants seldom stayed with her more than a few days—one woman lasted two weeks and spoke later of her experience as an ordeal. Many of those who knew her, including local tradespeople, and even some friends, considered her behaviour at times to be unreasonable. She found fault too easily and, as they saw it, often without cause. And her over-fussy personality was reflected in her small cluttered home, which had a place for everything with nothing out of place. So, when the unpolished thirty-year-old Kate entered the service of the excitable elderly Julia Thomas, trouble was almost certain to follow.

Kate Webster left her son in the care of Mrs Crease and took up her position as housekeeper at 2 Vine Cottages on 27 January. Despite Miss Loader's earlier high opinion of her, Kate turned out to be a very unsatisfactory servant, or so her mistress claimed. She was untidy in her work and often left jobs unfinished about the cottage, to the annoyance of Mrs Thomas, who constantly complained to friends of the incompetence and insolence of her Irish maid. For her part, Kate told Sarah Crease that she was living under great stress in trying to hold her patience and her tongue. No matter how hard she worked or however much she tried to please, Mrs Thomas persisted with her meddling interference and endless criticism. She was never satisfied with anything. How precisely the two women reacted to each other can only be guessed at but it seems certain that a clash of wills existed from the beginning, which built an unhealthy tension between them. Anyway, by mid-February, when Mrs Thomas could no longer endure the strain of their relationship, she gave her housekeeper notice to leave. It was arranged that Kate would quit her position at the end of the month.

There is support for the suggestion made by the Solicitor-

General at Kate's trial, that Mrs Thomas was actually afraid of her servant. She certainly approached several friends and appealed to them to come and live with her at Vine Cottages. If Kate had been intimidating her employer in some way then Mrs Thomas presumably felt less threatened with the arrival of a woman friend and her daughter who agreed to stay with her, at least until she had seen the back of her troublesome housekeeper. Events turned out differently.

Mrs Thomas's guests left Vine Cottage on Friday, 28 February, the same day that Kate Webster's notice expired. Kate did not leave with them. Instead, she asked Mrs Thomas if she could remain through the weekend, promising to remove herself and her belongings on Monday morning. Perhaps because everything had gone smoothly while her visitors were with her or, more likely, because she now considered her original apprehension to have been groundless, Mrs Thomas told Kate she could stay.

Nothing out of the ordinary happened on Saturday, and on the following day, Sunday, 2 March, the usual early-morning routine was followed, with Mrs Thomas going to church service at the Lecture Hall in nearby Hill Street. After lunch, as on previous Sundays, Kate was given the afternoon off, with the repeated instruction to return in time to allow Mrs Thomas to attend evening service, where she looked forward to meeting with friends. How Kate used her free time that day is not certain. Part of it, at least, she spent in The Hole in the Wall public house where, according to the landlady, Mrs Hayhoe, she took several drinks; she was very jolly but not drunk. Although she was already late, Kate left the pub for Vine Cottages still in the height of good humour, only to be confronted on her arrival by a furious Mrs Thomas, dressed for the street and seething with resentment at being delayed. A raging argument erupted on the doorstep. We do not know what was said but their angry exchange ended with Kate left at home to brood while Mrs Thomas, probably with some menacing remarks of Kate's ringing in her ears, rushed off to evening service, arriving, according to witnesses, in a very frightened or agitated state. Sitting just inside the door, she appeared nervous and distracted as she spoke with some members of the congregation. Unusually for her, Mrs Thomas did not wait for the end of prayers but left the service some ten minutes early and walked home alone. She was never again seen alive.

In the light of what went before it is hard to explain the decision of Mrs Thomas to return unaccompanied to Vine Cottages; it leaves unanswered some obvious questions: why, for instance, did she not ask her house guests to remain over the weekend? If they were not in a position to do so, why then did she not insist upon Kate's leaving on Friday? But, more than anything else, was it not strange, if she was in fear of the Irishwoman as seems certain, that she did not invite a friend home with her from church? Apart from some uncertain suggestions of suicidal tendencies in Mrs Thomas, her oddly indecisive behaviour was never satisfactorily explained.

In Kate's final confession, she said that Mrs Thomas came in from service and went directly upstairs. Kate immediately followed her and their violent quarrel of a few hours earlier was renewed with even greater intensity. In anger, Kate said: "I threw her from the top of the stairs to the ground floor..." To prevent her screaming Kate caught her tightly by the throat, and very soon the body of Julia Thomas lay still. To absolve herself of blame, Kate insisted she had been provoked and had acted on impulse.

But this sequence of events just did not tally with the evidence established by a reconstruction of the crime by the police. Bloodstains found in the bedroom and on a landing leading to it, together with the testimony of Mrs Jane Ives from next door, suggested a more savage end to the life of Mrs Thomas. The police were quite satisfied that Kate Webster followed Julia Thomas to her bedroom and there opened her skull with a meat cleaver. She then carried the corpse of her late employer downstairs and placed it on the kitchen table.

If some doubt surrounded the cause of Mrs Thomas's death, the horror which followed it is known with some certainty. Unless Kate Webster was insane, and no such plea was offered in her defence at her trial, what she did next defies rational explanation.

Taking an open razor, Kate first severed the head from the body. Then, using a meat saw and a carving knife, she butchered the remains of Mrs Thomas into manageably sized pieces, most of which she cooked in a copper boiler in the scullery. Entrails, some organs and other miscellaneous bits she consigned to the grate where they burned slowly on a roaring coal fire that she kept stoked throughout the night. Whether revolted by the violence of her own nature or exhausted by her hellish exertions, Kate decided to have a break. Her later admission that the strength of her resolution surprised her is surely an understatement. After a few moments' rest, when almost overcome by the nauseating stench, she forced herself to continue with the sickening task of dismembering her late mistress, when every impulse must have been to leave the charnel house and run away.

As daylight approached, Kate cleaned the kitchen. She cleared the grate, re-set the fire and, with other assorted portions, packed the cooked flesh from the boiler into a wooden box. The head of Mrs Thomas she parcelled separately in a sheet of brown paper. When she was satisfied that she had obliterated all traces of her incredible night's work, she found enough reserves of energy to undertake the usual Monday wash, giving the impression to neighbours that she was involved in her daily chores. After telling a lunchtime caller that Mrs Thomas was not at home, Kate probably rested; according to Mrs Ives, no further sounds were heard for the rest of the day. It is thought that Kate travelled about that evening, dropping the parts of the body which she had failed to cram into the box over a long trail between Richmond and Kingston. Only a foot was ever discovered.

If Kate was jaded on Tuesday morning, she never showed it. Nor did her remarkable energy flag under another long and exhausting day's activities. She was noticed at 6.30a.m. as she started her day, cleaning the front windows of the house. Later in the morning, Mrs Ives heard recognisable sounds as Kate busied herself with her regular household duties. In the late afternoon she went visiting.

While lodging in Hammersmith in 1873 Kate Webster had struck up a friendship with a family called Porter, who lived next door to her at 10 Rose Gardens. She often nursed a young daughter of theirs who was then a sick and frail child. The little girl, who had since died, was very fond of Kate, as indeed was the rest of the family. Explaining her move from the neighbourhood at the time, Kate told the Porters that she had found a job as a domestic cook in a large house in the Notting Hill area of London and promised to keep in touch. But, apart from a few visits back to Hammersmith, all contact ceased between them. Now, six years later, following the long absence and her unexpected reappearance, Kate was warmly welcomed by her friends when she arrived at Rose Gardens about 6.00p.m. that Tuesday evening. Invited to stay for tea, Kate placed a black shopping-bag she had been holding under the table as she ate.

Kate, genial and talkative, told Ann and Henry Porter that she had been married and widowed since last seeing them and that her husband, a Mr Thomas, was not long dead. The Porters expressed their sympathy. Kate then cheered them up with more exciting news. An aunt of hers, she said, had left her a well-furnished house in Richmond. The Porters expressed their delight. But, explained Kate, as her parents were anxious for her to return to Ireland, it would be necessary for her to sell the property. Before leaving, she asked Henry Porter if he would help her by finding an agent who would sell her house for her. He suggested she try some established firms in the Richmond district, as he knew nothing about such matters himself.

Kate persisted and seemed satisfied when he agreed to make some enquiries, at least about the disposal of her furniture.

Henry Porter offered to escort Kate back to the railway station. With his teenaged son, Robert, he took turns carrying her bag until eventually the trio arrived at the Oxford and Cambridge public house at the foot of Hammersmith Bridge. They had just settled themselves down for a few drinks when Kate surprisingly announced that she had to see a friend in Barnes. Promising not to delay, she picked up her shopping-bag and left the pub. When she returned soon afterwards, she was empty-handed. Gone was the bag and, with it, Mrs Thomas's head—or so the police later believed. She informed the Porters that she had met with her friend and now wished to return to Richmond, as it was getting late. At the station she persuaded Henry Porter to allow his son to accompany her home. Henry instructed Robert to be as quick as he could and not to dally.

It was now nearly eleven o'clock at night but Kate had not yet finished her day's travels, for she had yet another friend to meet. On reaching Vine Cottages, Kate told Robert that she had a box, "I want you to help me carry to Richmond Bridge." The box was heavy and unwieldy but between them they managed to get it to the bridge, where it was placed in a seat recess. Kate said that she would wait there for her friend and urged young Porter to go on ahead to the station where she would soon join him. He had gone only a short distance when he heard a dull splash from the river below, and almost immediately after, Kate emerged from the gloom, telling Robert that her contact had arrived and had taken charge of the box. At Richmond railway station they discovered that Robert had missed the last train, so they returned to Vine Cottages, where Kate made up a bed for her young companion. The following morning before sending him on his way, she fed him and gave him a large bag of assorted groceries to take to his mother. He hadn't long left when Kate followed him to Rose Gardens, once more raising the subject with Henry Porter of the possibility of selling her furniture. She did not return to Vine Cottages that night but stayed in Hammersmith with the Porters.

Police involvement in the Barnes mystery, as the newspapers would call it, began on the morning of Wednesday, 5 March 1879, when a man entered Barnes police station in West London to report a discovery he had just made in the River Thames. Henry Wheatly, a coal-porter, was on his way to work with a colleague when he noticed an object trapped in the mud near Barnes Bridge. Closer inspection showed it to be a lidded wooden box securely bound with a length of strong cord. When Wheatly cut through the binding with his pocket-knife, the sodden boards of the box fell apart, leaving the contents strewn on the river bank. Even then, the coalman was not sure what he had found. The box was filled with chunks of flesh; it looked like some type of butcher's meat but, if it was, Wheatly could not identify it. His first inclination was to leave his discovery where he had found it and continue on to his job but the thought that the flesh might be human changed his mind. Leaving his friend to stand guard over their curious prize, Wheatly strode off to alert the police.

The first officer to arrive at the scene from Barnes police station was Inspector George Harber. Accompanying him was Dr Jason Adams, a local physician who had worked with the police on other occasions. One glance was enough for the doctor to tell the inspector that the remains were human, though he could not be sure whether the pieces had come from one or more bodies. Adams was surprised to discover that much of the flesh had been cooked.

The gruesome mass was taken to Barnes mortuary, where it was later subjected to detailed examination by forensic pathologist Dr Thomas Bonds of Westminster Hospital. In his post-mortem account to the police, Dr Bonds reported the remains to be those of an adult female from which the head, a foot and some other pieces were missing. He confirmed Dr Adams's opinion that parts of the remains had been cooked and much of the body had been boiled in water. The pathologist established the height of the woman to have been a little over five feet and her age probably more than fifty. Cause of death was unknown, as was the identity of the lady.

Nearly all published reports of the post-mortem condemned the poor taste of medical students whom the newspapers were unanimous in blaming for putting the body in the river, though they did pose some questions. Why would medical students, or anyone else, go to the trouble of boiling part of the corpse and packing it, with uncooked portions, in a box before disposing of the lot in the waters of the Thames? And if it was a prank directed at the authorities by misguided students, surely they would have included in the box the most ghastly relic of all—the severed head? The press offered no explanations and readers were left to guess at the answers for themselves.

One young reader who was trying to make sense of things was Robert Porter. He read in the *Graphic* of 9 March the story of the body in the Thames, though his attention was more attracted to the account of the box, which seemed to the teenager to match the description of the box he had carried for Kate five days earlier. After some thought he dismissed the notion from his mind, believing the whole thing to be mere coincidence.

In the meantime, there was a good deal of toing and froing as Kate, now sleeping at Rose Gardens, made daily visits to Vine Cottages with some member of the Porter family in tow, all of them anxious to view her new acquisition. On Thursday, 6 March, William Porter, Robert's older brother, went to examine the house but first had to borrow a ladder and get in through a window because Kate could not find the door-keys. Their dilemma was observed and remembered. On Friday it was the turn of the mother, Ann Porter, to make a tour of the property. She strolled from room to room, admitting to her hostess that she was most impressed, even a little envious, with all she had seen on her visit. She left for Rose Gardens in jubilant mood when Kate promised her the contents of the kitchen. Tut-tutting Ann Porter's thanks, Kate explained that, while the house furniture would fetch good prices, kitchen equipment never realised its true worth at a sale.

Saturday afternoon saw the arrival at Vine Cottages of Henry Porter, who complimented Kate on the fine condition of the home she had been so lucky to inherit. After long asking, Kate finally drew a positive response from Porter concerning the sale of the furniture; he promised to take her to see a potential buyer the following day.

Good as his word, Henry Porter took Kate a few doors down Rose Gardens to his local, The Rising Sun, on Sunday, 9 March—the same day his young son Robert read about the discovery of human remains in the Thames—and introduced her to the licensee, John Church, as Mrs Thomas, who wished to dispose of her furniture before returning to Ireland. When Church expressed interest, arrangements were made for him to visit Vine Cottages to view the contents. Rarely can the sale of a few pieces of furniture have involved such extended negotiations as did the items Kate eventually sold to the publican. On Monday he called on Kate but no agreement was reached and a similar negative result followed on Tuesday, despite the helpful presence of Henry Porter, who seemingly acted as sort of mediating valuer. Another week was to pass before the deal was concluded, with Church offering £68 for the items he wanted and Kate agreeing to accept the figure after being given £18 as an initial deposit. Finally, about 7.00p.m. on Tuesday, 18 March, Mr Henry Weston, the Hammersmith greengrocer engaged by Church, pulled up outside Vine Cottages, ready to move the furniture.

With Porter's help John Church had just loaded a few items into a van when events took a dramatic turn with the sudden appearance of Elizabeth Ives, who wanted to know from Weston what was happening. He told her he had instructions to take furniture to Hammersmith. It was luck that prevented Kate's exposure there and then. She was in a state of near shock when, overhearing this conversation, she quickly cornered her neighbour and told her that Mrs Thomas was disposing of her belongings. Kate, visibly unnerved, told a surprised Miss Ives that she could not give her her employer's address because she did not know where she was. Far from satisfied with that response, Miss Ives said she would make some enquiries and then returned to her own house, banging the door behind her.

In view of the amount of traffic to her neighbour's door it is surprising Elizabeth Ives's curiosity did not spur her to action a lot sooner. In the fortnight since Mrs Thomas had died, the Porter family had been traipsing in and out of her house, sometimes arriving or leaving at unusual hours, while Church in a matter of nine days had been back and forth about a dozen times in the protracted haggle over prices. When it is considered she had also witnessed, with her mother, the episode of the ladder, which she later admitted she thought suspicious, it is a wonder Miss Ives's inquisitiveness did not get the better of her.

John Church, who was still clearly under the impression he was dealing with Mrs Thomas, could not make head nor tail of what was going on. He suspected, though, that someone else had a prior claim to the goods he had bought, probably the excited woman who had just left. So, to avoid any trouble, he ordered his helpers to bring back into the house the pieces they had earlier removed. When everything was returned to its place, Kate, who was very agitated, rushed into the house and reappeared moments later, carrying a bundle of dresses which she threw into the back of the nearest van. Later that evening, they were delivered to The Rising Sun, placed in a spare room at the back of the pub and, for a time, forgotten. Church, fuming over Kate's suspected duplicity, went with Porter and Weston, and his driver, to discuss the strange happenings of the evening over a few drinks.

When the men left with the vans, Kate's calm control deserted her with the realisation that time was against her. As she became more alarmed, the increasing need to distance herself from Vine Cottages led her to make a hasty decision, though it is almost certain that matters would not have ended differently had she decided to stay where she was and brazen it out. Saying only that his father wished to see him, Kate collected her son from the Porters' home about 10.00p.m. that Tuesday night and did a moonlight flit.

For a while Church was uncertain what to do but the next day he called on Miss Ives with Porter, hoping she might clear the air. For reasons which became plain later, she refused to talk with them. But two days later on 21 March events began rapidly unfolding. In a pocket of one of the dresses left at The Rising Sun Church's wife, Maria, found a letter addressed to Mrs Thomas from a Mr Charles Mehennick of Finsbury Park. John Church and Henry Porter went to see him. Mehennick, a long-time friend of Mrs Thomas, immediately contacted her solicitor when he realised the sinister implications of his visitors' story.

On Saturday morning, William Hughes, brother of Mrs Thomas's executor, travelled to Hammersmith to interview Church and Porter and was concerned enough with what he heard that all three went to Richmond police station to express their fears for Mrs Thomas. The trio then went to 2 Vine Cottages with Inspector John Pearlman, who forced an entry and made a superficial search of the premises. Nothing suspicious was found. When the inspector called to The Rising Sun the next day, he heard from Church of Robert Porter's experience with Kate and her box. After questioning by Pearlman, Robert accompanied the inspector to Barnes and identified the box he had carried with Kate. This information brought the police in force to Vine Cottages on Monday morning, where a more thorough search yielded some interesting discoveries. They retrieved fragments of bones from beneath the scullery boiler and a razor, a cleaver and some partly burned clothing from the coal-cellar. These

discoveries, together with bloodstains in the kitchen and in
the upper storey of the house, led police to circulate a
description of Kate, whom they wanted on suspicion of
murder. Four days later, on Friday, 28 March, Kate Webster
was arrested at the home of her uncle in Killane, Co
Wexford, and charged the next day at Enniscorthy police
station with the murder of Mrs Julia Thomas.

On her journey back to London, Kate insisted she was
innocent and asked the escorting officers, Inspectors John
Dowdale and Henry Jones, if anyone else had been arrested
for the crime. They strongly advised her to remain silent
until she arrived in Richmond. They were not at all surprised
at the statement she made when they got there. At Richmond
police station, on 30 March, Kate immediately accused
John Church of the murder, claiming she was his mistress
and in terror of him. Her allegations, cunningly contrived,
mixed fiction with facts the police might reasonably be
expected to know. She explained her readiness to dispose of
the body and conceal the crime by saying she was far too
frightened of Church to refuse. Church, she alleged, had
threatened to end her life just as he had ended the life of Mrs
Thomas, by stabbing her. Kate more or less introduced
herself into the case as a helpless accomplice. Her plausible
story was believed. In spite of his protestations, the
unfortunate Church was charged with the murder of Mrs
Thomas and stood with Kate before the Richmond
magistrates the following morning.

During the preliminary hearings which dragged on into
the middle of May, Kate's lies about Church became more
and more incredible. Luckily for the publican, who denied
everything, reliable witnesses were able to account for his
movements at the crucial time. He was discharged by the
magistrates as having no case to answer. When confronted
with Church's denial of her story, Kate responded in
characteristic fashion by telling another one. In the new
and amended version, marked by as many contradictions
and inconsistencies as were contained in her earlier recital,

Kate declared that Henry Porter had taken an active part in the murder. But Porter's alleged involvement in the crime was easily disproved and, despite her efforts to embroil as many people as possible, Kate alone was committed for trial for the murder of Julia Thomas.

The case for the Crown was presented by the Solicitor-General, Sir Hardinge Gifford, when the trial opened before Mr Justice Denman on 2 July 1879. The unenviable task of defending Kate was assigned to Mr Warner Sleigh.

In his opening address, Sir Hardinge told the jury that, although the head had not been located, they would have no doubts as to the identity of the remains or the box in which they were discovered when they had heard all the evidence. Neither would they have any doubt that Kate Webster murdered Mrs Thomas.

Naturally, much of the incriminating evidence came from John Church, the Porter family and the medical experts, Drs Adams and Bonds. Their evidence, together with supporting police testimony, formed the basis of the Crown's case against Kate. Solid as the prosecution's position appeared, they introduced additional evidence to clinch their argument. One witness who had a damning piece of information to impart was Mary Durden, who knew Kate when they both lived in Kingston. The accused, whom she met on 25 February, told her that she had been left a house and other property by an aunt who had recently died in Birmingham. To dispel any doubts about the premeditated nature of the murder, the Solicitor-General pointed out to the jury that this statement had been made almost a week before Mrs Thomas was last seen alive. In cross-examination, Mr Sleigh suggested that she was mistaken about the date but Mary Durden was an unyielding witness who refused to retract any part of her testimony.

One after another the witnesses came and went, with Kate's slim chance of acquittal going with them. Elizabeth Ives told of speaking with Weston and her refusal the following day to speak with Church and Porter because she remembered them, she said, and considered them fellow conspirators of Kate. Her mother, Mrs Jane Ives, who, it was reported, viewed her involvement in the trial with distaste, swore that no shouting match, as described by Kate, could have occurred without her hearing it. She was emphatic that on the night of Mrs Thomas's death a single loud noise was all she heard. It occurred at about 8.00p.m. and sounded like a heavy chair being overturned, she said. This sound, the prosecution claimed, was the victim's body striking the floor after being felled by the accused with a chopper.

After the reading of Kate's statements to the jury and the clarification of some points by recalled witnesses, the Crown rested its case.

The single most troublesome detail of the prosecution's case was the absence of positive identification of the remains. When Sleigh claimed in opening Kate's defence that the murder of Mrs Thomas had not been established, he seized on this one obvious weakness. The accused, he said, was being charged with the murder of a woman who could not in fact be shown to be dead. He reminded the jury that, when asked how the woman had died, Dr Bonds could not explain the death because there was no physical evidence to account for it. She could, as far as anyone knew, have died of a heart attack. And what was to be made of Dr Bonds's assertion that the remains which he examined were those of a female of over fifty years, while Dr Adams, speaking about the same corpse, believed it to be that of a woman between the ages of eighteen and thirty?

Referring next to the Crown's two leading witnesses, John Church and Henry Porter, defence counsel ridiculed the claim that they were ignorant of Kate's true identity. Then, denouncing Church's alliance with Kate as corrupt and intimidating, he warned the jury against accepting this witness's improbable story. Nor did he place any trust in Porter's claim that Kate's behaviour had never aroused suspicions until the moment of her disappearance. Sleigh scored some telling points off the medical experts; yet, in spite of his outspoken disdain for the evidence of Church and Porter, he failed in cross-examination to discredit their testimony.

Finally, Warner Sleigh spoke of Kate's kind and benevolent disposition, citing her love for her son, which, said her counsel, was absolute and unquestioned. He also mentioned her devotion to Porter's daughter during the child's illness but really there was not much he could say in her favour. With the barest of material, Mr Sleigh made a determined attempt to save the life of his client but, despite his best efforts, he could do little to alter Kate's murderous image and nothing at all to diminish the heinousness of her crime.

On Tuesday, 8 July, the trial went into its sixth and final day. Most of the morning's proceedings were taken up with the Solicitor-General's closing speech to the jury, which followed much the same course as his opening address of 2 July. The one point he did underline was the complete innocence of any wrongdoing of both Church and Porter. After telling the jury that the Crown had proved its case conclusively, he demanded they bring in a verdict of Guilty against Kate Webster for the wilful murder of Julia Thomas.

Following the lunchtime recess, Mr Justice Denman commenced a three-hour summing-up of the evidence. There could have been little doubt in anyone's mind by the time he had finished his review at 5.10p.m. as to his belief in her guilt. The first thing he told the jury was that, apart from any other consideration, Kate Webster was the one who impersonated Mrs Thomas and this, surely, had suspicious implications. After referring next to Kate's constant lying and how she had sought to divert suspicion from herself by involving others, the judge instructed the jury to ignore the suggested involvement of Church and Porter, both of whom had been most helpful to the police. Mr Sleigh, he said, in his eagerness to establish the innocence of his client, had offered Church and Porter as alternative culprits but no evidence introduced during the trial supported this contention. Ending his summation, the judge said that the prosecution had made a formidable case but if members of the jury had any doubts about its merits, then the benefit of such doubts must be given to the accused. The jury was then led from the courtroom to start their deliberations, which lasted just over an hour. They returned with the guilty verdict everyone had expected.

When asked if she had anything to say before the court pronounced sentence, Kate, in a stumbling recital, spoke vaguely of a past filled with sorrow and misfortune. She was still denying her guilt when the judge sentenced her to death.

The trial, which lasted the best part of a week, had no highlights. While the Crown's case had the value of simplicity, Kate's defence was a series of improbabilities complicated by lies. No real surprise was expressed at the final verdict; questions were asked only about the motive for the killing. Xenophobic publications had no difficulty in solving the puzzle; for them Kate's very Irishness was reason enough for the savagery of her behaviour. But even more moderate elements of the press thought Kate's staring eyes, prominent teeth and even the shape of her head were clear indications of her brutish and subhuman nature. The truth may be that she killed Mrs Thomas during a period of alcoholic mental derangement. Whatever her motive, Kate Webster, one of the most vilified of Irish murderers, was hanged for her crime at Wandsworth Prison at 9.00a.m. on 29 July 1879.

4

THE CUMBERLAND STREET
TRAGEDY

Robert Butler   Dunedin, New Zealand, 1880

In Dunedin, New Zealand, in the early hours of Saturday, 13 March 1880, the home of solicitor James Stamper was burgled. The thief, who stole several small items including a pair of opera-glasses, set fire to the house, burning it to the ground. The solicitor and his family barely escaped with their lives. This crime, which stunned the community, was soon eclipsed by the discovery the following morning of a more horrific outrage, one that caused an instant sensation.

At half past five on Sunday morning, Charles Robb, a householder of Cumberland Street, noticed smoke coming from the single-storey cottage of a neighbour, James Dewar, a butcher. Robb roused his son James and together they ran to the scene of the fire, gaining entry to the cottage by the back door, which they found wide open. Choking smoke filled the interior, forcing young Robb to crawl on his hands and knees down the small passage to the Dewars' bedroom, where he found a body almost directly inside the door. It was Mrs Dewar. She was still alive but had been savagely beaten about the head and seemed beyond medical aid. Robb dragged her into the passage, returning to the bedroom to extinguish the fire with the help of his father. There, when the smoke cleared, he recognised the body of James Dewar, upon which marks of violence similar to those suffered by his wife were clearly visible. On the bed beside Dewar lay the body of his nine-month-old daughter. As far as Robb could see, the dead infant bore no outward signs of violence. He also noticed near the bed a bloody axe and beneath the bed a candle which the murderer had obviously used to start a fire in the bedclothes.

Leaving his son at the cottage, Charles Robb rushed off to report the tragedy to the police. Inspector Frederick Mallard was sent to take charge of the investigation, and arrangements were made to have Mrs Dewar removed to hospital. She never regained consciousness, and died late on Sunday night.

As the morning wore on, extra police arrived at the house in Cumberland Street and a thorough search was begun. The Dewars' bedroom was first examined and there officers found the door, walls and bedclothes heavily bloodstained. Brain matter was also discovered on two of the walls nearest the bed and on a pillow and coverlet, clear evidence of the brutal ferocity of the attacks. Elsewhere they found a window open and on the sill was the outline of a nailed boot. There were no signs of robbery and no other clues were found.

Inspector Mallard's next move was to have his men canvass the immediate area, in the hope that a neighbour might have noticed something suspicious, but nobody had anything helpful to tell the police. The scope of the investigation was then extended to include the examination of residents of all cheap lodging-houses, small hotels and hostels in Dunedin. Particular attention was to be paid to clothing. The police believed, naturally, that the murderer could not have carried out his crime without getting his clothes badly stained with the blood of his victims.

What looked like the first break in the case came on Sunday evening, twelve hours after the discovery of the murders, when Detective Constable John Bain, on one of his last calls of the day, visited the Scotia Hotel in Dundas Street. Here he learned of the odd behaviour of a Mr Robert

Butler, who had been staying at the hotel and left that morning. A maid, Sarah Gillespie, told Bain that Butler had come to the hotel on Thursday, 11 March. She remembered his arrival quite distinctly. Butler, she recalled, was wearing a dark purple check suit. Sarah went on to tell the detective that Butler slept in his room on Thursday night and, although he remained in the hotel on Friday, he did not use his bed that night. She did not see him again until twenty minutes to seven on Sunday morning, when she opened the front door of the hotel to find Butler standing in the street.

According to the maid, Butler was white in the face, trembling and appeared to be nervous, glancing over his shoulder as if he had been followed. After paying his account, he went to his room, collected a parcel which he had with him when he booked in, refused breakfast but drank some beer, and then left the hotel, still in an agitated state. For Bain, Butler's actions might mean anything or nothing to the enquiry, but later that Sunday night the whole incident took on a particular significance, when he learned of the strange conduct of a man at another hotel some miles from Dunedin.

Later investigations showed that on his departure from the Scotia Hotel, Butler walked the short distance to Leighton's shop at the corner of Castle and Dundas Streets. When he got no answer to his knocking, he continued as far as Cumberland Street, where he was seen to look in the direction of Dewar's cottage. After spending only moments at the kerb, he returned to Leighton's shop which was now open and bought five tins of salmon. Butler then made his way to the Botanical Gardens, where he left an empty salmon tin beneath a seat, and then went on to the Town Belt—a hill overlooking Dunedin—where he disposed of two further empty tins and some items of stained clothing.

Shortly after 10.00p.m. that night, Butler arrived at the Saratoga Hotel in Waitaki, some twelve miles from Dunedin, and went straight to the dining-room. Here, he was seen to be listless and at one time appeared to be sleeping but when

SEAN O'BRIEN

the Cumberland Street tragedy was mentioned by the proprietor, Mr Coleman, Butler became positively active. Unable to relax, he walked about, and when he did sit down he moved restlessly in his chair. Clearly uneasy in company, he seemed impatient to leave the hotel, which he did immediately after a hastily eaten supper. Guests at the hotel had no idea, of course, who the stranger was but they thought his conduct odd enough to encourage the hotel-owner to notify the police. The visitor's general appearance and suspicious behaviour seemed to correspond in some detail with that of the man described to detective Bain by Sarah Gillespie. A warrant was issued for his arrest.

The wanted man was not again sighted until the afternoon of Tuesday, 16 March, at Waikonaiti, about fifteen miles from Dunedin, where he was approached by two uniformed constables. Both policemen would later testify at the preliminary hearings that Butler, after some conversation, jumped backwards, drew a revolver from his pocket and pointed it in turn at each of them. Butler would emphatically deny the accusation. He was merely handing over the gun when he stumbled, he said. One way or the other, he was disarmed, and lodged in the Waikonaiti lock-up, where he was searched. Taken from him were a pair of opera-glasses, forty-six cartridges, a few coins and two tins of salmon, "corresponding in every particular with those purchased at Leighton's shop." A curious feature of Butler's dress at this time was the absence of the outer soles of his boots. Also missing was a moustache which he was known recently to have grown and the backs of his hands were noticeably scratched.

Later that evening, Inspector Mallard arrived in Waikonaiti to interrogate the prisoner. Butler admitted to stealing the opera-glasses from Mr Stamper and to setting fire to his house but repudiated all suggestions that he had been responsible for the deaths of the Dewar family. Despite his protestations, Butler was held in custody and charged with murder. At the coroner's and police courts he was found to have a case to answer and was committed for trial to the Supreme Court at Dunedin.

The shock and terror the Dewars' deaths provoked was without precedent in Dunedin's history and it was beyond the town's understanding how this ordinary family could have aroused such deadly malice. The crime had been committed with vicious and horrible brutality, prompted by no discernible motive, and, so far as anyone could judge, without the slightest gain to the murderer. There was endless speculation and widespread curiosity about the reason for the killings, and Butler, who had already been tried and convicted a thousand times in people's minds, was expected to throw much light on the mystery of Cumberland Street at his trial.

Robert Butler was born in Co Kilkenny, Ireland, in 1845. Little is known of his early life. He referred only rarely to his youth and even then never with any useful details. In conversation with an acquaintance in Melbourne, he said, "...in matters of education I have had but the briefest skirmish." This remark, like much else that Butler said, cannot be taken as the whole truth. He had obviously had some basic schooling for he worked as a journalist in Melbourne, Australia and Dunedin, and for a time managed his own school in Otago, New Zealand. But those were irregular intervals in a life spent mostly in jails. He arrived in Australia from Ireland when he was fifteen years old and of the following sixteen years he spent thirteen of them in prison. His crimes included vagrancy, theft, burglary and highway robbery. His criminal career continued after his arrival in New Zealand in 1876, culminating in his arrest for the murder which he was staunchly denying when he stood trial for his life before Mr Justice Williams on Thursday, 8 April 1880.

The case against the prisoner was presented by the Crown Solicitor, Mr B Haggitt. Butler caused noisy excitement in the public gallery and probably surprised the jury too when he told the court he was going to conduct his own defence. The judge's response to this announcement was: "I can only say that I am sorry you have adopted that resolution." Before the trial opened, it was generally acknowledged that the outcome could be forecast without difficulty. Now Butler's decision to defend himself seemed to make this prediction a certainty. Robert Butler was confidently expected to end his life at the end of a hangman's rope.

From early on the morning of the first day of the trial the enormous interest in the case was evident. Outside the court an excited and barely controlled mob of outraged citizens had waited for hours for a glimpse of Butler, while inside, the building was jammed to suffocation as bailiffs and constables tried in vain to clear corridors as the prosecutor opened his address.

In traditional fashion, Haggitt in his statement detailed what the Crown expected to prove, outlining Butler's movements from the time of his arrival at the Scotia Hotel on 11 March until his arrest on 14 March. He told the jury of the discovery of the victims' bodies and described the nature of the wounds inflicted upon them: five axe-blows to the head of James Dewar, for whose murder Butler stood accused, and three axe-blows to the head of Dewar's wife, Elizabeth. The infant daughter had died of suffocation, he said. There was a host of suspicious circumstances pointing to the guilt of the accused, the prosecutor went on. He laid great emphasis on the fact that Butler had attempted to shoot dead, or seriously maim, the constables sent to arrest him. Why would he do such a thing? Because the prisoner had already murdered and was prepared to do so again to avoid capture. The court next heard how Butler, on more than one occasion before 11 March, had suggested to Inspector Mallard, whom he knew well, that setting fire to a premises after a burglary would be an excellent way of destroying incriminating evidence. For the second time within an hour, an excited buzz was audible throughout the courtroom. But prosecutor Haggitt could have excited very few of those crowded about him with the Crown's next submission on that first morning of the trial.

This, in part, is how the prosecutor explained to the jury his reasons for believing why Butler had slaughtered the butcher and his wife: "Why did the prisoner select this house—a house of this kind—if his object was plunder, when there were other houses wherein he was so much more likely to get something worth taking than he was likely to get in a house of that description?...I say it was a proper place for a person seeking money only to enter. A person wanting money only would enter just such a place as that occupied by the deceased. The houses of persons in a large way of business—the houses of merchants or businessmen—could no doubt be as easily entered and with a better chance of plunder of value, but money, which the prisoner stood in need of, he would be less likely to find in such a house than in the house he chose. People who occupy large houses and who fill better positions than the deceased keep their money, if they have it, in banks and not in their houses. Although in saying this it is not necessary that the Crown should suggest a motive for an offence of this kind—it is not necessary that a motive should even be suggested to you."

Viewed from any standpoint, this really is an extraordinary statement. The effect of its recital to the jury can only be imagined. It is likely that the jurors were bemused rather than enlightened after listening to it, and it is certainly probable also that Mr Haggitt's cavalier disregard of motive bewildered them still further. What nobody knew but, more than anything else, what everyone wanted to know, including members of the jury, was the reasons for the killings. Why would Butler, or anyone else, want savagely to murder the butcher and his wife? Crown counsel might have been wiser to tell the jury that the motive for the murders was unknown but that the case against Butler would still succeed on the strength and persuasive nature of the prosecution's evidence and the

SEAN O'BRIEN

credibility of the witnesses who would present it. Haggitt's assertion that the Crown need not prove, or even suggest, motive was correct in law but juries do expect commonsense explanations. In this instance, they were subjected to a tedious and unnecessary story of such improbable features that it can have done little to advance the Crown's case.

The prosecutor said he had very little more to say. Would the members of the jury agree that there were sinister implications to the removal of the prisoner's moustache? Haggitt thought they would. Butler had also removed the soles from his boots; did they feel, as he did, that this was a suspicious act in view of the odd imprint found on the windowsill at Cumberland Street. He was certain of their agreement on this point too. And, he said, he had no doubt in his mind either that, when they heard the evidence of the Crown's doctors concerning bloodstains on the prisoner's clothing, they would be satisfied that the guilt of the accused had been conclusively established. In the light of later events, this was a curious final remark.

Only a couple of witnesses were called before the midday recess. The reason for calling the first of them, Mary Grant, is now obscure. She said she cleaned the Dewars' knives every two or three weeks and a knife found in the cottage garden did not correspond with any of them. The next witness, James Nickolson, a draughtsman, came from the Survey Office with an armful of maps and drawings relating to various locations referred to in the charge and dryly explained their relevance before the jury was rescued at 1.00p.m. when the court rose for lunch.

When the hearing resumed Haggitt briefly examined Sergeant Shirley of the Dunedin police. Then, in answer to a question put to him by Butler in cross-examination, the witness said that apart from some ruffled clothes in a drawer, there were no signs of disturbance. To a further query, he replied that the rest of the house showed no evidence of disorder or disarray. These were valuable admissions to have on record. If nothing was stolen and robbery could be ruled out as a motive, what reasonable hypothesis remained?

There then followed a parade of prosecution witnesses, each one giving support to various aspects of the indictment. Their evidence did not vary in essential details from that which they had given in the lower courts. The Robbs appeared to tell of their part in the discovery of the murders, George Leighton recalled selling salmon to the prisoner and James Youngman, a ranger on the Town Belt, explained how he found two salmon tins and the bloodstained purple suit. John Wadsworth, identifying himself as a milkboy, said he saw Butler looking down Cumberland Street towards Dewar's cottage on Sunday morning; a tramcar driver, William McGuire, told how he saw Dewar walking in the direction of his home on Saturday night and Richard Howard, Dewar's employer, spoke of the deceased's kind nature and upstanding character. When Sarah Gillespie was called, she repeated, with slight variations, the story she had told Detective Bain.

The two most important witnesses of the day were the two policemen who had arrested Butler, Constables Golborne and Townsend. But, unlike the previous witnesses, their testimony was to depart dramatically from their earlier statements made at the preliminary hearings. While they were now uncertain of the substance of their conversation with Butler, they were decisive in their recollections of the prisoner's behaviour when he was asked to accompany them to the police station. Did they still believe that he had threatened their lives with his revolver, Butler wanted to know from Townsend.

"I was under the impression at first that you moved it from one hand to the other but I have been thinking it over and, from a conversation I had with the other constable, I think not."

When Constable Golborne supported the testimony of his colleague, Butler must have been heartened, for the evidence of the officers could hardly have been more explicit. Although this testimony was already implied in their answers to Mr Haggitt's rather vague questioning, the new picture of the prisoner's capture still surprised the court. Mr Justice Williams, probably as surprised as anyone else, lost track of time and did not bring the first day's proceedings to a close until well past seven in the evening.

If Butler reflected on his first day's efforts to save his own life, he was likely enough pleased with the results. He had extracted two significant admissions from prosecution witnesses which must have cast doubts on at least part of the Crown's argument. Sergeant Shirley swore that no evidence of robbery was discovered at the scene of the crime and the policemen sent to arrest him now testified that he had made no threatening gestures nor had he caused them any trouble. The case against him was still formidable but, by the valuable points he had scored, Robert Butler, defence counsel, managed to attract as much attention as Robert Butler, the accused.

The second day of the trial opened with the testimony of Inspector Mallard. The inspector told the prosecutor how Butler had acknowledged his part in the fire at the Stampers' house. Despite his repeated denials of the capital offence, Mallard said he charged the prisoner with murder because of Butler's suspicious conduct after the crime, his refusal satisfactorily to explain his whereabouts on Saturday night and because of a series of conversations he had had with the accused in the weeks preceding the crime. Much of their talks, the inspector said, centred on Butler's suggestion of how easy it was to destroy all trace of crime by fire.

These remarks would have sounded sinister when Inspector Mallard repeated them from the witness-box; at that moment Butler's case must have been severely damaged.

In his cross-examination of the police inspector, Butler asked a total of thirty-four questions, most of them relating to the odd fact that the inspector took no notes while interrogating him but wrote a memorandum of the interview from memory, several hours afterwards. Butler was scathing in his criticism of the policeman's work, especially so concerning the inspector's approach to him after he had been formally charged. Would the inspector like to explain to the jury why he continued to question the prisoner even after he had been charged, Butler asked. Mallard's reply, vague and not too convincing, related to the difficulty of speaking and writing at the same time. The disclosure that questions had been put to the prisoner after the charge had been made brought censure, not only from Butler himself but from a brusque Mr Justice Williams: "You mean to say you asked him those questions, Mr Mallard, after you had arrested him and charged him with the murder? It seems to me to be a highly unusual course for a police officer to pursue."

This rebuke was little more than a gentle slap on the hand for the inspector and did not materially change his evidence. Butler, though, by deft questioning, had steered the jury's attention away from the more ominous features of the inspector's evidence and centred it instead on irregularities of police procedure. For such a potentially damaging witness Butler probably thought his handling of Mallard was satisfactory, for he had managed to dilute to some extent the strength of the inspector's testimony. Just the same, he must have been relieved to see the back of Inspector Mallard as he left the witness-box to make way for Detective Bain.

Detective Bain had little to add to the sum of the Crown's case. The high point of his evidence came when he mentioned the hotel maid's description of Butler's dark purple check suit. The prosecutor in his opening statement had the prisoner "dressed in a dark lavender suit with a small check on it." Nicety of distinction aside, the jury may have thought it a strange disguise for a man who, if the Crown counsel was to be believed, was about to embark on an orgy of theft, arson and murder. After taking a middle course in his questioning of Bain, Butler released the detective without either benefit or loss to his defence, and the next man to hold centre-stage for a moment was the foreman of the jury, William Quick. The foreman told Mr Justice Williams that the jury wished to inspect the murder site. Instructing the sheriff to accompany the jurors to Cumberland Street, the judge adjourned the trial until 2.00p.m.

The remainder of the second day's hearing was taken up with the evidence of the Crown's team of three doctors. Dr Brown told of examining the bodies of the victims, and he and Drs Alexander and Hocken described their findings after a study of the Dewars' bedroom and the prisoner's clothes. The condition of the bedroom and its late occupants was already well known. Focus of interest now lay with what many observers believed was the most damning accusation so far advanced by the Crown: that Butler's bloodstained suit and shirt would prove his guilt as the killer of James Dewar. It was an unwarranted assumption.

The prosecution's mistaken trust in the positive nature of the police evidence of arrest had already caused problems under Butler's cross-examination. Now further complications were about to emerge for the Crown Solicitor.

For the benefit of judge and jury a frightening and gory picture of the carnage at Cumberland Street had been painted by Haggitt in his opening speech; the jurors themselves had made a chaperoned pilgrimage to the infamous cottage to view the preserved bloody evidence and the Crown's medical witnesses had sworn to the presence of blood on the coat, trousers and shirt of the prisoner. Overall, this seemingly comprehensive catalogue suggested a blood-drenched murderer. But this image assumed a different complexion on examination and by mid-afternoon it was clear to all that the prosecution's case was not going according to plan.

At one point the prosecutor halted in his examination of Dr Brown to address the bench in an interchange that tells us something about the state of forensic science in 1880 and even more perhaps about the state of the Crown's case against Butler.

"Would Your Honour allow the jury to use a magnifying glass in looking at the clothes?"

"I can see no objection, although it might not help them much."

"I can show Your Honour that it will make a wonderful difference to use a magnifying glass."

"I see no particular objection…the jury will be able to see the exact position of the blood spots."

Continuing his evidence Dr Brown said he received the prisoner's coat for chemical and microscopic study and found one spot of blood on the left lapel and another on the right lapel. A further spot was discovered on the edge of the lining of the left sleeve. An incredulous Mr Justice Williams, not bothering to excuse himself, interrupted to ask:

"What was the size of the spots on the coat?"

"The one on the left lapel was larger than the others, being about the size of the head of a match, while the others were about the size of a pin's head."

After some further questions concerning the trousers and the shirt, the judge finally said: "I will simply put it this way. Were the spots so minute that an ordinary person would not have noticed them?"

"They were."

On the subject of blood there was no more to be said, it seemed. But there was more. Dr Alexander and Dr Hocken corroborated the evidence of their colleague Dr Brown and, despite lengthy and vigorous questioning on re-examination, Haggitt failed to alter the testimony of his own experts on the amount of blood discovered on the accused's clothes. That they agreed that Butler could still have committed the murder was an irrelevance, for Mr Justice Williams, in the space of a dozen or so questions, had eroded the substance of the Crown's medical evidence and left the prosecution's case in disarray. To add to the discomfort of the Crown, all three doctors agreed with Butler's suggestion while under cross-examination that the bloodstaining of his clothes could just as easily have been caused by the scratches on the backs of his hands.

The doctors were the last witnesses called by the Crown Solicitor and their evidence, which brought the second day's hearing to an end, failed completely to support the curiously extravagant description by the prosecutor of Butler as the blood-soaked killer.

It was now Saturday, 10 April, the third day of the trial. In its opening moments on Thursday, the court had heard Robert Butler sensationally announce he would act as his own counsel. Saturday's proceedings got under way with another piece of news that was hardly less spectacular. Haggitt told the jury that he was not in law bound to review the evidence for them, and he would not do so.

If the jury pondered the implications of the prosecutor's peculiar decision, did they see it as a sportsman's levelling of the odds or as a tacit, if curious, acknowledgement of the frail character of the Crown's case?

At ten minutes past ten, Robert Butler entered into a marathon closing address of almost six hours' duration. Allowing for the difficulties of the prison regime under which he had to prepare his case, Butler's painstaking and exhaustive analysis of the evidence against him was a superb achievement.

In summarising the Crown's case, he said the prosecutor claimed that his talks with Mallard prior to the murders, his demeanour after them, his sudden disappearance from Dunedin, his bloodstained clothing and his unexplained movements on Saturday night all added up to an indication that he was the murderer. He would answer all these allegations, he promised, and expose the obvious weaknesses and extraordinary contradictions in the prosecution's argument. But first he had this to say to the jury: "Gentlemen of the jury, this is a case wholly of circumstances which has been brought against me mainly by the fact that I was once before guilty of a crime, which at the time I frankly acknowledged. It had evidently been assumed at once by the police that I was the guilty man!" Having placed the blame for his predicament on police prejudice, Butler advised the jury to be most careful in their examination of circumstantial evidence, more especially when there was not a particle of direct evidence to support it. In all cases like this one, he said, it was of the greatest import, where the result could mean life or death, that they be not only certain in their minds that he was guilty, but equally certain that nobody else could possibly be guilty. His explanation for directing his own case was a simple one, he told the jury. He was not prepared to leave his life in the hands of any stranger.

Butler first attacked the prosecution's case by discrediting its witnesses and casting doubt on their memory and credibility. Much of the Crown's evidence concerning his general conduct he denied but, if he did behave oddly, he attributed this to the fact that he was bothered by the crime he had committed at Stamper's house. Every aspect of the Crown's argument was riddled with holes, he said. Take, for instance, the evidence of the milkboy—how could any witness swear that he, Butler, was looking at any particular house while glancing down a street? Wadsworth's claim was a foolish one. And what were they to make of the maid's evidence? She said he was nervous and trembled but when Leighton and Wadsworth saw him only moments later he was calm and composed, not trembling at all. The best that could be said for her was that she spoke on her oath rashly and carelessly. And, far from running away, had he not been seen shopping and observed while loitering at the pavement by several people? He was either loitering or absconding and in his view the prosecution had not made up its mind what he was doing. The evidence of those at the Saratoga Hotel who swore that while he was there he was agitated and anxious to leave amounted to a contradiction, for the same witnesses also said that he remained to eat a full supper before he departed the premises. What was to be said for the credibility of these people? The Crown had made much of his presence in the neighbourhood of the crime but, suggested Butler, the same could be said of many people. Saturday night he spent wandering the streets. He could be no more explicit, he told the jury, because of his drunken condition brought on by depression and a consciousness of his wrongdoing at the home of the solicitor. With emphasis he reminded the jury how remarkable was the retraction of the earlier evidence of the arresting constables. Could they recall clearly the policemen saying that he had done absolutely nothing to hinder them in their duty? They must remember this, Butler instructed, because the prosecution had included it as a vital element in its case against him. His purple check suit, he declared, had become very wet and badly soiled from his travels in the rough countryside and that was why he had thrown it away. He added offhandedly, and there seems little reason to doubt him, that he had no special fondness for it. The bloodstains found on this suit resulted, he explained, from the many cuts and scratches he received from thorny bushes in the Town Belt and elsewhere. He then made the point that Inspector Mallard's account of their previous conversations was selective in that they had discussed many aspects of crime, criminals, criminal behaviour and the whole question of punishment, not just the matter of firing a premises as a means of destroying incriminating evidence. He next told the jury that he removed the soles from his boots simply because the leather was broken and caused him discomfort in walking. Coming to the end of his address, Butler, who had already shown a flair for the dramatic, emotionally informed the jury that he had killed nobody and asked permission to put on the purple suit to prove his point. Allowed to do so, he quietly explained that conclusions arrived at by the prosecution were not correct. By indicating to the jury the location and the slight amount of staining, Butler impressively demonstrated that it would have been almost impossible for him to have murdered two people with an axe while dressed in the suit he was now wearing. Then, speaking with greater intensity, Butler concluded: "I will be content to trust that when you, gentlemen of the jury, have examined the evidence as carefully as the doctors profess to have examined the blood spots, you will think it far more safe that you should trust your own senses and intelligence than to be led by the nose by the doctors."

Long before anyone set foot in the courtroom on Thursday morning, when his trial began, Butler had precisely nothing in his favour, not even vague doubt as to his guilt. Newspapers throughout New Zealand were convinced that he was a murderer. The police believed so too. The public, deeply angered, were in agreement and simply no one thought Butler had even a leg to stand on. But, after trusting his life to his own unproved skills, he had created—with the help of some curiously sloppy Crown evidence— uncertainties in the mind of at least one man, Mr Justice Williams.

In his summing-up, which was favourable to the prisoner, the judge pointed to many of the weaknesses referred to by Butler in the prosecution's case and underlined one very obvious flaw. That the accused was seen near the scene of the crime meant nothing, said the judge. In a town of 40 000 persons this could hardly be described as an exclusive opportunity. Whatever else Haggitt had succeeded in proving, he had not, according to Mr Justice Williams, managed to place Butler at the murder site, and that was the crucial failing in his argument. This opinion was, in essence, a rejection of the Crown's presentation.

The jury, after three hours' deliberation, agreed with the judge and returned a verdict of Not Guilty.

Unfortunately for Butler, securing an acquittal where a conviction seemed inevitable did not gain him his liberty. Later at the same sessions he was sentenced to eighteen years' imprisonment for burning the residence of James Stamper.

He came out of prison in 1896 and returned to Australia,

where almost immediately he was in trouble with the police. Of two offences he successfully defended himself on a charge of highway robbery but, because the evidence against him on the second indictment was indisputable, he pleaded guilty, leaving himself at the mercy of the court. On 18 June, Mr Justice Holroyd at the Melbourne Supreme Court sentenced Butler to a term of ten years with hard labour for breaking into a hairdresser's shop—even for those times, a terribly severe punishment.

In 1904 Butler left prison for the last time. He worked for a while as reporter on the *Melbourne Argus*, before moving to Sydney and eventually to Brisbane, Queensland. There, the *Brisbane Courier* in its issue of 24 March 1905 reported:

"Toowong was the scene of a sensational occurrence last night. A man named William Munday being bailed up on one of the principal highways was dangerously wounded. His assailant, who was unknown to Munday, made good his escape and up till a late hour last night he had succeeded in evading the police."

Later that night William Munday died from a bullet wound but not before he had identified Robert Butler as the man who had shot him. Butler, who seemed to be in a stupor when arrested, said he was James Wharton and under that name he was charged with the murder of William Munday at the Supreme Court of Brisbane. Although on this occasion he was defended by counsel, it did him no good, for he was found guilty and sentenced to death by hanging on 30 June 1905.

In spite of many thinking it deserved, it was a sad end for a man who seemed capable of living a more productive and fulfilling life. Years spent in prisons had taken their toll on his health until he was little more than an invalid awaiting his fate. But if this second trial for murder brought about his death, the charge of killing James Dewar in Dunedin provided him with an incredible courtroom triumph over enormous odds and, as far as we know, it was the only worthwhile achievement in the otherwise wasted life of Robert Butler.

5

SHE HAD SO MANY CHILDREN

Sarah Jane Robinson   Boston, USA, 1888

Interest in a murder is usually transient, though occasionally a case comes along that instantly attracts and holds the public attention. No one can explain this. A trial which seems to contain all the essential ingredients to satisfy a curious public may go unheeded, while another unlikely case will suddenly explode into stop-press news, catching everybody by surprise. Two murderesses who operated within six years and two hundred miles of each other illustrate this point very well.

In Fall River, Massachusetts, on a sunny August morning in 1892, Lizzy Borden butchered her father and stepmother with an axe. Lizzy was arrested and charged with murder. After a pantomime trial she was acquitted. Americans were shocked by the jury's verdict. And no wonder. As the song very properly admonishes: "You Can't Chop Your Momma Up in Massachusetts." But compared to the murderous career of Ireland's Mrs Robinson around Boston between 1881 and 1886, Lizzy's romp with her hatchet was little more than a misdemeanour. Yet a century after her trial the name Lizzy Borden is known to everyone; no one has ever heard of Sarah Jane Robinson. Her anonymity is remarkable—a word used constantly to describe the whole Robinson saga. Opening the second case against her, District

Attorney Stevens told the jury that they had "entered upon the trial of one of the most remarkable cases in the history of criminal law that has been tried in Massachusetts..." And her own lawyer, Mr Goodrich, in coming near the end of his closing argument, said of the case that "the most remarkable feature is the absence of any evidence that the accused ever had in her possession the alleged means of death." Not to be outdone, Judge Knowlton told the jury in his summing-up: "Everything in this case is remarkable." Some of it was indeed but most remarkable of all was Sarah Jane Robinson herself.

Even so, despite her infamy and all that was said about it, and the acres of newsprint that analysed and described it, Mrs Robinson remains a mystery.

In the first week of August 1886 the situation was no different. Apart from a handful of mystified doctors and some very disillusioned moneylenders, few people had ever heard of her, and her barren existence would have passed totally unnoticed had she not sent for a doctor just one time too often.

Mrs Robinson's son William (or Willie as he was usually known) was a member of an insurance cooperative, and when he became ill in August, his mother sent for its medical officer, Dr White. Although he had passed off earlier rumours as foolish, the doctor was immediately suspicious. From his own knowledge, he was aware that Willie's sister, Elizabeth, had died as recently as February, and while doing his rounds he had heard stories of strange deaths of other close relatives of Sarah Jane, all of whom had surprisingly succumbed to the same mysterious ailment. To establish the exact cause of Willie's sickness, Dr White had Professor Wood of Harvard medical school examine a sample of the patient's vomit. While this was going on, Willie's condition worsened and he died. Two days later, when the Harvard professor reported the presence of arsenic in the submitted sample, Sarah Jane Robinson was arrested and charged with murdering her twenty-three-year-old son.

Shortly after Willie's death the activities of Sarah Jane began to engage the leisurely and combined attention of the Boston, Cambridge and Somerville police forces. By the time the trial opened they had reams of depositions, though most of them had little apparent relevance to Willie's poisoning. Their evidence, too, proved to be of small help to the prosecuting attorney. Overall Mrs Robinson's trial was badly prepared and poorly presented by the prosecutor. Several opportunities of suggesting guilt were lost in the cross-examination of certain witnesses, and the final speech was full of inconsistencies, containing a host of disjointed and uncoordinated statements that so confused the jury they were unable to reach agreement. The result was a mistrial. In reviewing the case for its readers, the New York *Sun* described the prosecutor's cross-examination of Mrs Robinson as "slow, rambling and pointless" and his address to the jury as "full of hot air."

Considering the amount of publicity the case had generated, it was a great embarrassment to the Commonwealth when it failed to secure a conviction against Sarah Jane. But she was not retried for Willie's death. Instead she was held in custody and as a result of a mass of further discoveries, belatedly made by the police, she was again charged with murder, this time for the poisoning of her brother-in-law in 1885.

Mrs Robinson's trial for the murder of her rather splendidly named brother-in-law, Prince Arthur Freeman, opened before Judge J Field and Judge J Knowlton on 6 February 1888 in the Supreme Judicial Court of Massachusetts, Cambridge. The Commonwealth, leaving nothing to chance, brought in its biggest guns, Attorney-General AJ Waterman and District Attorney William B Stevens. Sarah Jane was defended by Mr John Goodrich, who had with him as associate counsel Mr David Crane.

Although it was to seize the attention of America and dominate front-page headlines across the nation, Mrs Robinson's six-day trial got off to a slow start.

The twelfth man had just been empanelled when the jury was quickly ushered from the court to the jury-room. Some questions of law which counsel wished to argue in their absence was the reason given to the jurors for their abrupt removal. With the jury-box empty the district attorney made his submission.

The prisoner, he said, had been indicted for murdering her brother-in-law, Prince Arthur Freeman, on 27 June 1885, by poisoning him with arsenic, and he would bring forward evidence directly related to that charge. But he wished also to introduce further evidence which would tend to show that on 26 February 1885 Mrs Robinson poisoned her brother-in-law's wife, her own sister Annie Freeman, also by the administration of arsenic, and that on 23 July 1886 she killed her sister's son, Thomas Freeman, arsenic again being the instrument of death. The Commonwealth wanted to introduce evidence of those other deaths for the reason that each death was part of a single scheme conceived by Sarah Jane Robinson as far back as February 1885.

In other words what the district attorney was saying was that Mrs Robinson had, in February 1885, formed a plan for killing her sister, her sister's husband and her sister's child. Unlikely as it seemed, it was a single transaction influenced by a single motive and designed to accomplish a single objective.

And the motive? That was next explained by William Stevens. As he saw it, the motive was to obtain two thousand dollars insurance money made payable by Freeman to his wife Annie in the event of his death. The prisoner believed, contended Stevens, that with her sister dead Freeman could be readily persuaded to sign over to her the insurance money, and it would then be only a matter of killing him to get her hands on it when the right moment came along.

Stevens's stark vision of Sarah Jane as a multiple murderess, made the more shocking by his matter-of-fact delivery, chilled those listeners not already half-frozen in a bitingly cold courtroom that February morning. Appropriately, the day was one of the coldest ever recorded in Boston.

When Goodrich rose to reply for the defence he was immediately critical of the district attorney's presentation. He told the court that he disagreed strongly with Stevens's submission and argued vehemently against the inclusion of any testimony that did not have a direct bearing on the death of Prince Arthur Freeman. The prosecutor, he claimed, was trying to bring before the court a great deal of evidence which was outside the rule of law. Goodrich complained bitterly that the Commonwealth was putting on his client the duty of defending herself on three charges when she had been called upon to answer but one. Anyway, it was not reasonable to assume, as the prosecutor had, that Mrs Robinson had any interest in the death of Mrs Freeman, for her sister's death would not have left her one bit nearer the insurance money. As she was not an heir to the estate she would not have benefited by the death of Mrs Freeman or by the death of Mr Freeman. The prisoner had no more claim to the insurance money than a total stranger, and to allow the admission of evidence which might suggest otherwise would be greatly to prejudice the minds of the jury against Mrs Robinson. Goodrich closed by calling the district attorney's case pure fantasy. The judges disagreed with him and the Commonwealth prevailed. Judge Field told counsel that evidence of Mrs Freeman's death would be admitted as it tended to show that it was part of a plan or scheme, though evidence of the death of her son Thomas would not for the present be heard but might later be introduced by the Commonwealth when the case was better understood.

Sarah Jane's case was then opened to the recalled jury and the trial started in earnest.

All of what had been said before the bench was now repeated and examined by Stevens. The district attorney told the court that about 1853 Sarah Jane Tennant came to

Boston with her ten-year-old sister, Annie, from Newtownhamilton in Co Armagh in Ireland. She was fifteen at the time. In Cambridge, some five years later, she married Moses Robinson, a wheelwright. Robinson died in 1882, leaving her with five children. Annie, in the meantime, had also married and in 1885 was living in South Boston with her husband, Prince Arthur Freeman, and their two children, an infant, Elizabeth, and six-year-old Thomas. Freeman, a general labourer without savings, made some provision for his family in case of his death by joining a mutual benefit society, the United Order of Pilgrim Fathers. He insured his life with the society for two thousand dollars. Soon afterwards Annie became ill.

A doctor who was called to examine Annie Freeman in the middle of February 1885 said she had pneumonia but would recover with proper attention—and she did improve for a while. She was making good progress when Mrs Robinson arrived in South Boston to supervise her sister's treatment, dismissing a nurse who was already there. Within a couple of days, despite the comforting presence of Sarah Jane, Annie's condition worsened, with symptoms not previously noticed, and on 27 February she died in agony. Curiously, even while Annie's condition was stable and at a time when her doctor thought she had improved considerably, Sarah Jane was telling neighbours her sister would never get well. This, said Mr Stevens, was information that nobody else seemed to possess.

Nor were they the only curious statements she made. On the day of Annie's funeral—and even before it—she asked several friends and neighbours to bring pressure to bear on Freeman to get him and his family to come and live with her because, said Stevens: "She was one of the most extraordinary women, I venture to say, that ever lived and knew that when she brought him under her influence it would be an easy matter to have that insurance assigned to her." Well, maybe...Her brother-in-law and his children did go to live with Sarah Jane—though the baby survived only until

April—and he did assign the insurance money to her for the purpose of taking care of young Tommy, should that need arise. And it did after 27 June, when Prince Arthur died in an agonising and puzzling way after Sarah Jane had several times prophesied the death. But according to William Stevens, his death was no longer a puzzle. Sarah Jane poisoned him and just three months later, on 22 September, she received her two thousand dollars. That money had been her goal and, concluded the district attorney, she had poisoned two people to achieve it.

It was already four o'clock in the afternoon when the district attorney ended his address to the jury, but six witnesses were still to be heard before Judge Field called a halt to the proceedings. It was a gruelling first day in a freezing courtroom and the days that followed were just as long and exhausting, suggesting that the judges were anxious to bring the trial to a brisk conclusion.

It can be guessed, too, that the Commonwealth saw Sarah Jane as a continuing embarrassment to be tidied away as quickly as possible.

The early prosecution witnesses endorsed some of the claims made by Stevens. One of them, Mrs Susan Marshall, said that she met Mrs Robinson when she called to Mrs Freeman's home on 25 February. She admitted to Stevens that in a conversation that day Mrs Robinson had made a rather curious statement.

"What was it?"

"She remarked she did not expect that Annie would ever get better or ever leave her room."

The witness then told the district attorney that Mrs Robinson later asked her to use her influence as a friend to "...advise him [Freeman] to come and live with her."

Judge Field interjected to enquire:

"She asked you this, when?"

"She asked me about two hours after Annie stopped breathing."

The remaining witnesses that day, including Freeman's

sister, Mrs Catherine Melvin, had very similar stories to tell, although there was no doubt which one of them created the biggest stir. It was Mrs Mary Wright, who lived in rented rooms in the same tenement as the Freemans. Answering a question of Stevens, Mrs Wright recalled Sarah Jane's telling her that she thought she should come to take care of her sister, "as she had a terrible dream and she knew her sister would never get any better; and that whenever she had a dream like that there was always one of the family died." Mrs Wright was also present, she said, when Sarah Jane entered her sister's sickroom, closing the door behind her. When she returned she told her visitor, "There, I have fixed it all now; any little rings or anything that Annie has I have had her distribute so that there will be no trouble if anything should happen to her." Journalists in the courtroom who had trekked from all over America to cover the case were unanimous in reporting that this witness's evidence of Mrs Robinson's dreams and subsequent family deaths, and her talk of distributing her dying sister's property, greatly shocked the jury. Those first-day witnesses retracted nothing of their evidence when cross-examined by Goodrich for the defence.

And for the defence, the second day of the trial began as badly as the first one had ended. As early as 10.00a.m. the signs were already there that John Goodrich—who shared with St Jude a reputation as a succour in hopeless cases—would have to produce something miraculous if he was to save his client from conviction. His chances were not great. Goodrich, although a hugely respected and experienced criminal trial lawyer, was not without defect. One acknowledged fault, an obvious one, was a brittle temperament. It showed itself soon enough and as the trial progressed he became increasingly irritable with witnesses. But on that second day he was to display the far more serious fault of not knowing when to stop asking questions.

When the district attorney's first witness, Belle Clough, confirmed she was an intimate friend of Mrs Robinson's daughter Lizzy (Elizabeth) and was a regular visitor at the Robinson house where Freeman and his two children were then living, Stevens started off by enquiring into the relationship that existed between the two families. It was a bad one, according to the witness. They argued a lot and Mrs Robinson was always speaking against her brother-in-law, saying he was a lazy good-for-nothing and of no use to her because the little bit he earned he spent on cab fares; she also said she wished he could have died instead of her sister. The district attorney next wanted to hear about a particular conversation she had heard when she was having a meal with Lizzy and Mrs Robinson.

"Mrs Robinson said she wished someone would give him [Freeman] a dose and put him out of the way. Then she stopped a minute, then she got real nervous and looked over her shoulder, and we thought she was going to fall. Lizzy said, 'What is the matter, Mother, has Father come to you again?' She said, 'Yes, I thought your father touched me on the shoulder.' Lizzy said, 'Oh this is Father come for Uncle, Mother.' Her mother said, 'Yes it is, I should not wonder but something would happen to your uncle soon.'"

The introduction into the evidence of visitations from the dead was an unexpected bonus for the newspapers and they made the most of it. So, of course, did Stevens. He had the witness recount how Lizzy Robinson had often told her that, shortly before a member of her family was "called over," her mother would first receive a warning from a visitor from the other side, usually an earlier deceased Robinson.

John Goodrich very wisely started his cross-examination of Belle Clough by tiptoeing gingerly around the most damaging parts of her evidence, first asking harmless questions about how long she had known the Robinsons— "Eight years"—and how she got along with Mrs Robinson— "Fine." Counsel then suggested to the witness that although Mrs Robinson and her brother-in-law may have had minor differences of opinion, "Her conduct towards him was always kind and affectionate?"

"Yes sir. When strangers were around."

With the impatience that was to become familiar in future days, Goodrich snapped at the witness:

"My enquiry was whether it was always kind and affectionate."

"No sir, not always."

This answer was not much to Goodrich's liking either, and he said so, but still persisted with the subject. Questioning the young witness at length about Mrs Robinson and her brother-in-law, he tried to establish that a friendly family atmosphere had existed between them. He made no headway. All he achieved was the reiteration of Belle Clough's damning evidence, including her insistence that "Mrs Robinson often felt her dead husband touch her on the shoulders whenever anyone was called away; soon after that they died."

The purpose of the evidence of the district attorney's next series of witnesses was to corroborate earlier testimony of Mrs Robinson's eerie accuracy in prophesying family deaths and to let the jury hear how she persistently badgered society officers for the handing over of Freeman's two thousand dollars' insurance money.

Mrs Florence Stanwood, a collector with the United Order of Pilgrim Fathers, related how, after Annie's funeral, Mrs Robinson prevailed on her to advise Mr Freeman to alter his will in her favour in case anything should happen to him and she would be left to look after his two children. Mrs Robinson also made enquiries of this and other officials to ensure that Freeman was keeping his policy payments up to date. Mrs Stanwood continued that when Prince Arthur died, he was in debt to the society to the amount of 75 cents, but because she took pity on Mrs Robinson she paid this sum herself so that Sarah Jane would not be deprived of benefit. Little thanks she got for her compassion. Because certain society rules and legal procedures had to be followed, there was some delay before payment could be made to Mrs

The execution of William Burke in Edinburgh, January 1829
(pp 1–19)

The representation of Kate Webster at Madame Tussauds
(pp 38–56)

Albert D Richardson, victim of
Daniel McFarland (pp 20–37)

Robert Butler, murderer of
Mrs Dewar (pp 57–74)

Mrs Charlotte Bryant
(pp 102–123)

Frederick Bryant's cottage

Dr John Bodkin Adams (pp 157–175)

Dr Adams being escorted from Kent Lodge after his arrest

Robert Clements with his fourth wife, Amy, after their wedding in 1940
(pp 124–139)

Frederick Emmet-Dunne, convicted and stripped of his military stripes
(pp 140–156)

Patrick Byrne, the accused
(pp 176–191)

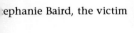

ephanie Baird, the victim

THE ANNEXE—
MURDERED GIRL'S
ROOM WAS HERE

IRONING-ROOM:
GIRL WAS
ATTACKED HERE

Scene of the Stephanie Baird murder, the YWCA Hostel at Edgbaston

Robinson. While she was waiting, she was constantly demanding and abusive, giving no thanks to the many members of the society who had tried to help her.

The doctors were next to appear. The first of them, Dr John Nichols, was called by Stevens to tell what he knew of Annie Freeman's death. The jury heard nothing new; Nichols merely repeated what the district attorney himself had told them in his opening address. When Annie was getting better she suddenly got worse and died. It all seemed straightforward enough but the evidence was not quite so clear-cut when John Goodrich had finished his cross-examination of the doctor.

With jurors and witnesses alike, Goodrich favoured the sweep-them-off-their-feet-immediately approach and that was exactly how he opened his questioning of Dr Nichols.

"By the way, what did you certify to be the cause of death?"

"I was extremely puzzled to know what to certify."

"Won't you tell us what you did certify in the first place?"

"As I remember, I certified disease of the stomach."

"Were the symptoms consistent with disease of the stomach?"

When counsel got the doctor to answer yes, he abruptly dismissed the witness, having scored a valuable point for the defence.

Dr AJ Davidson, who had consulted with Nichols on Mrs Freeman's illness, contributed no new facts to the case and was quickly followed by Professor William Hills. The professor confirmed for Stevens that he had examined several of Annie Freeman's organs and discovered traces of arsenic in them all in sufficient quantities, he believed, to have caused her death.

When it was Goodrich's turn to cross-examine the witness, he used the opportunity to launch a new theory. In his questioning of Nichols, counsel suggested that Mrs Freeman's death might have resulted from natural causes.

After all, the doctor had issued a death certificate specifying disease of the stomach; now, maybe predictably, he wished to explain how arsenic had managed to get into the dead woman's body.

John Goodrich entered into a long conversation with Hills about the preserving of corpses and sought from the professor information relating to the various techniques and substances used in the process of embalming. After a while came these few questions and answers which converted Professor Hills into the most effective witness yet for the defence.

"Would it be safe to draw any conclusion whatever from the presence of arsenic in the body, if it appeared that the body had been treated with embalming fluid?"

"I think not."

"And for what reason?"

"Because I know that, ordinarily, embalming fluids contain arsenic, the substance under investigation."

There then followed a number of less important witnesses, including undertakers and cemetery workers who told of collecting and burying the bodies of Annie Freeman and her husband. All of their evidence was of a formal nature and beyond challenge but Goodrich still had some questions for them. It was immediately clear why. His questions related to the condition of the coffins and the state of the ground into which they were placed. He later used this information to doubtful effect, suggesting that arsenic in the surrounding sodden earth had seeped through the broken caskets and into the bodies of the Freemans. As an explanation, it was refreshingly novel; the experts thought little of it.

Goodrich had a difficult and unpopular case to defend and it was not easy going for him. Some of his questions had a certain desperation about them and at times became bogged down in irrelevancies. An instance of this was when he asked Winslow Litchfield, superintendent of Garden Cemetery, what he did when he received Mr Freeman's body for burial. The unsurprising reply, "I buried it," brought a buzz of amusement from the spectators and further upset Sarah Jane's counsel. But, generally, he performed well with poor material.

The jury certainly had its work cut out to keep track of the argument, for the evidence seemed to be moving in circles. Only an hour after describing his post-mortem findings on Annie Freeman's corpse, Professor Hills was back in the witness-chair, this time to explain what he found when he delved into the innards of Prince Arthur. Arsenic. And off they went again, with prosecution and defence duplicating most of the evidence already produced on Hills's first appearance. But, true to form and almost inevitably now, Sarah Jane's chief counsel had another new theory to be aired. He wanted to know from the professor what the likely effects would be on a person working closely with strong chemical detergents. Although Hills had few facts to impart on such a vast subject, Goodrich claimed that Freeman could have been fatally poisoned after inhaling the fumes from a tank of sulphuric acid while descaling metal parts at his workplace.

If variety and choice were what you were after, then Goodrich was definitely your man; with him the possibilities seemed limitless.

On the third day of the trial, the moneylenders had their say. The district attorney called five of these witnesses and none had favourable recollections of Mrs Robinson. On another point they were also unanimous. All had engaged in financial transactions with Sarah Jane but none had profited from the experience. In each instance she borrowed sums ranging from $40 to $100, offering her furniture as security. But she moved frequently, making her difficult to trace, and when she was located she offered excuses, rarely money. To frustrate the money men further, when a sheriff's officer called on her with a repossession order, the pledged furniture was always missing.

Daniel Desmond, one of these witnesses, told Stevens of

making a loan of $75 to Sarah Jane in September 1883 and the torment he suffered afterwards. Although she had given him a false name—Mary Allen—and changed her address several times, he eventually found her but her misfortunes prevented her from making any repayments. On subsequent visits she spoke to him of family deaths. When Desmond's evidence started to ramble, Judge Field intervened: "State what you said and what she said, in substance."

"I said, 'It is very singular you have so many deaths in your family; can it be possible?' She said, 'Yes I think I shall lose them all; I think they will all die, all go the same way.' I said, 'What appears to be the matter with them?' She said, 'I think they are in a general decline.'" As an exercise in understatement her last remark could hardly be bettered.

Sarah Jane then hinted mysteriously at some money she was expecting and told Desmond, "I am going to be all right shortly; I can see my way clear now." She repaid the moneylender in October 1885, two years after the loan was made and a fortnight after receiving her insurance benefit.

Daniel Desmond was the last of the prosecution's key witnesses and his dismissal brought to a close the government's case, after Goodrich failed to get the broker to alter his testimony.

It was David Crane, Goodrich's associate, who made the opening speech for the defence. Following standard procedure, he at once reminded the jury of the terrible responsibility which rested upon them and asked that they approach their great task with clear heads and honest hearts.

Crane's early outline went over much of the ground covered by Stevens in his opening presentation. The jury had again to listen to the story of Sarah Jane's arrival in America from her home in Ireland, her marriage to Robinson, her support of her five children after his death and Annie's fatal illness. From there Crane's interpretation of events differed radically from that of the district attorney and he started by emphasising that it was in response to a direct request from Freeman that Mrs Robinson went to South Boston to care for her sister. After Annie's death her great concern was for the welfare of her sister's children, and that was why she had asked Freeman to come with his family to her home. He was happy to do so. But tragedy followed them and in April the baby died after being sick for a short time. Subsequently Mr Freeman took ill and he also died. The prisoner was now charged with his murder.

Reminding the court of Professor Hills's evidence—that, because of the use of embalming fluids which contained arsenic, there was no certain way of knowing how the poison had entered Freeman's system—Crane added, "I do not know whether he died of arsenical poisoning or not. We have no means of telling."

Then Crane asked a whole series of questions after first pointing out that if stolen goods were found in the possession of a person, that person would have to explain how he came by them. "Pray tell me what Mrs Robinson has to explain. Did they find the means of death upon her? Did they find arsenic in her possession? Did they find that she talked about it, ever dealt in it, ever purchased it, had any books treating upon it? Did they find any vials in the house, anything of that kind? She has got nothing to explain. There is nothing she can explain." Stirring stuff! Then doing some explaining of his own, David Crane said that there were other theories about the case that were more consistent, and vastly more reasonable, than the one suggesting that the prisoner had killed Freeman. He was about to introduce another player into the courtroom drama. "I will state right here, that there was a character by the name of Beers, Dr Beers." According to Crane, Sarah Jane had known Beers for years, but lost track of him after she married Robinson. They met again in 1884 and the doctor soon became a regular visitor to her home. He was infatuated with her and wanted to marry her. "He was there mornings, nights and Sundays; for days, weeks and months. Wherever she went this Dr Beers appeared." He was there constantly during Mrs

Freeman's illness, and very significantly, said Crane, he brought medicine there. He was persistent in claiming Mrs Robinson's hand in marriage until it transpired "much to her surprise, chagrin and mortification, that Beers was there merely for the loaves and fishes, and that he had left a devoted wife."

It was not difficult to guess what the latest defence strategy would be. Crane's first group of witnesses testified briefly to Sarah Jane's compassionate nature and the depth of her religious fervour—qualities hitherto unmentioned—while Charlie, her nineteen-year-old son, swore to his mother's affectionate relationship with Freeman. But in real terms, and certainly as far as the American press was concerned, Goodrich produced only one witness in Sarah Jane's defence and that was Sarah Jane herself.

Over the first three days of the hearing and a succession of often damaging witnesses, Sarah Jane Robinson remained impassive, showing no signs that she was anything more than another spectator at the trial.

She retained her poise under examination by her own counsel, who saw to it that his client suffered as little wear and tear as possible on the witness-stand. His questions skimmed along over the events in her life until he arrived at the period of Annie's final illness. Earlier, on the first afternoon of the trial, Mrs Susan Marshall gave evidence of visiting the patient, and while there meeting a Dr Beers. With an assurance that would not have been out of place in the hills of Connemara, Beers handed Sarah Jane a bottle with the words: "You will find that strictly pure." Now Crane was asking: "Mrs Robinson, do you remember Dr Beers calling at Mrs Freeman's during her sickness?" The district attorney, who did not need penetrating insight to see where Crane's questioning would lead, was on his feet objecting, but Goodrich insisted that conversations between Mrs Robinson and Dr Beers were relevant and essential to his case. There was a good deal of legal argument from both sides before Judge Field said that if it was shown that Mr

Freeman and Mrs Robinson were attentive to each other, and if it was shown that Dr Beers was jealous of Mr Freeman, there might be a state of fact that could be termed competent evidence. He then told counsel that the defence could show that Dr Beers had easy access to both Mrs Freeman and Mr Freeman.

Thanks to that legal wrangle, Dr Beers was now established as an important personality in the case and, in Judge Field's view, he was also a person with the possible motive of jealousy for the elimination of Prince Arthur Freeman. The defence could not have hoped for anything better.

When Sarah Jane eventually confirmed for Crane that Dr Beers had brought medicine for Annie and had visited her each day during her illness, counsel quickly turned to the fatal sickness of Freeman. Here Mrs Robinson's evidence was a little different: Dr Beers, she said, was a regular caller and had brought medicine to the patient, but she admitted she did not know if Freeman ever took it; she knew nothing about it. And that about summed up the total of her evidence to her counsel. As best she could she cared for the Freemans in their sickness and was always at their beck and call but knew nothing whatever about their deaths.

Goodrich and Crane could not have been displeased with their client's performance.

When Sarah Jane was taken over by Attorney-General Waterman for cross-examination, she often sought refuge in the age-old reply: "I can't remember." But she was just as calm and confident a witness as she had been earlier when telling her story with the guidance of her own counsel. Her resolve never wavered nor did she enmesh herself in contradictions or illogical explanations. When asked a question she simply answered it or said she could not remember. During her questioning by a very disgruntled Waterman, there were no high points, no emotional outbursts, no fiery arguments across the courtroom. In fact there was very little of anything—and that includes evidence.

Mr Waterman's cross-examination of Mrs Robinson was quite positively numbing in its duplication, repetition and reiteration, and must have acted as a powerful anaesthetic to those assembled in the courtroom.

To give a brief glimpse of Waterman's style, and some idea of the torture it inflicted on the jury, a small part of the exchange requires quotation. It is important too, because it explains, at least in part, why Waterman failed to extract any incriminating admissions from the prisoner and why, after four hours of cross-examination, Mrs Robinson, without effort, got the better of the Commonwealth's Attorney-general:

"Did you see Mrs Marshall at the time your sister was sick?"

"Yes, sir."

"See her there?"

"Yes, sir. I sent for her."

"You saw her there?"

"Yes, sir."

"Did you have a talk with her there, anything about Prince and the children?"

"Yes, sir. I think I did."

"About their going to live with you?"

"Yes, sir."

"You talked there."

"Yes, sir."

"How long had you been there then?"

"I couldn't tell you."

"You were there about a week in the whole before your sister died, weren't you?"

"I couldn't tell you just how long it was."

"Can't you tell the day you went there to take care of her?"

"Yes, sir. I went there on a Monday."

"And she died the following Saturday?"

"No, sir. She died on Thursday the 26th."

"Then would you say you were there only part of one

week?"

"No, sir. I don't think so. I think that I was there. I am quite sure I was there one Sabbath with her."

"Well, are you sure about it?"

"Well, I am quite sure about it."

"Then you were there ten or twelve days?"

"I don't know how many days; I only know the day I went there, the day she died."

"What is the day you went there?"

"On Monday."

"Now can't you tell whether you were there on more than one Monday?"

"No, sir. I can't."

"You can't tell whether you were there ten days or four days?"

"No, sir. I can't. I haven't got the dates."

"You went from RH Whites; you were there at work at the time?"

"Yes, sir."

"Did you go there to stay the first day you went there?"

"No, sir."

"Did you go there the first time you went there on Monday?"

"No, sir. The first time I went there was on Friday evening."

"Did you see your sister that evening?"

"Yes, sir. I did."

"You didn't stay during the night?"

"No, sir. I only stayed a short time."

"You went home."

"Yes, sir."

"Did you go on Saturday?"

"No, sir. I did not."

"On Sunday?"

"No, sir."

"On Monday?"

"Yes, sir."

"On the following Monday?"

"Yes, sir."

"Why didn't you go there on Saturday and Sunday?"

"On Saturday I had to go back to my work at the store."

"When did you see Mrs Marshall there at your sister's? When was the first time you saw her there?"

Full circle.

This extract is typical. There is much more, and all of it just as stupefying; for ineptitude, it defies comparison.

After the sensation caused by Willie's murder and the shocking revelations confidently expected to emerge from her cross-examination at her second trial, Sarah Jane Robinson was a huge disappointment to spectators and public alike. Throughout the hearing she sat immobile, staring straight ahead with her face rarely changing expression. She was always courteous when she spoke but gave her evidence in a voice that never varied in tone or volume. She never hemmed or hawed but neither did she offer spur-of-the-moment replies. She volunteered nothing, at the same time giving the impression she was trying to be helpful, which no doubt she was. No matter what was suggested to her or said about her, her response was always the same, a polite aloofness. With apparent ease and without missing a step, she led the Attorney-General round and round the mulberry bush.

But while Mr Waterman failed to puncture Sarah Jane's calm exterior, it is doubtful that a more skilful questioner would have fared any better. She was so unconcerned with her predicament as to seem to be uninvolved in the trial. She was a cipher, colourless as a glass of water.

If Sarah Jane was not high on the list of sensations at her own trial, the same could not be said for the next important witness to take the oath.

Whatever the demands of justice, given the choice, no lawyer with tuppence worth of sense would have produced Dr CC Beers to testify for either side in any courtroom proceedings. But, of course, the Attorney-General had no choice. Although Waterman had already rested the Commonwealth's case he was forced into the move to rebut Goodrich's claim that Beers could have killed the Freemans just as easily as could Mrs Robinson.

Charles Clinton Beers was a great one for talking, and during the week of the trial it was impossible to stop him. He affected an air of joviality and indicated his self-importance with a loud voice. When not giving evidence, he entertained groups of newspapermen with lively quips and stirring accounts of his colourful life. But in or out of court he said whatever came into his head and had answers for everything, including questions he was never asked. He was neither a calm nor a neutral source of information and often seemed to be vying with counsel for the court's attention. Glorying in the spotlight, his noisy personality dominated much of Thursday, the fourth day of the trial, and engrossed America's readers for days afterwards.

The district attorney decided to get the worst of it over as soon as possible. He started by asking Beers a few awkward questions about himself and queried some of the weakest parts of his evidence in an attempt to offset the effect of Goodrich's certain attack on the same vulnerable points. From the beginning, Stevens's task was hopeless.

First Beers admitted that he had spent five years in jail in Connecticut "on a charge of burglary which I never did." Then, with a kind of perverse pride, he blurted out the information that together with Sarah Jane he had been arrested for the murder of Willie Robinson. Locals were aware of his early involvement in the case, but it was news to the rest of America. (Beers never stood trial for Willie's killing because of lack of evidence.)

Anything he could say after that was going to be anticlimactic. But Beers, never a witness to omit quaint details, told how he started work with his father as a trouser-cutter, but quickly tired of the job and decided to become a dentist. Dentistry too had to take a back seat when he discovered he "had a mesmeric power whereby the application of my hands could relieve disease and I practised that." Women more than men, he explained, appeared to benefit from his ministrations. Beers, as the defence had already insinuated, was a bit of a dab hand with the ladies.

Where the present case was concerned, he denied giving medicine to any member of the Robinson family and rejected suggestions that he had any romantic interest in Mrs Robinson herself. Although she was full of sweet talk, he closed his ears to such blandishments, informing Stevens that his relationship with her had been "strictly spiritual." At that uplifting comment the district attorney handed over the witness to the opposition to make what they could of him. Stevens, though, already knew what was coming.

The defence was determined that now was the moment to take the trial by the scruff of the neck and cut Beers down to size at the same time.

Notable among Goodrich's questions was his first:

"Dr Beers, are you under indictment in this court for the murder of the prisoner's daughter, Lizzy?"

"I am."

Pandemonium.

"Silence, silence!" roared the bailiff but few took any notice of him. And who could blame them? They had never heard anything like it before in their lives.

It must have been a dramatic day in the Cambridge courthouse. There was Beers boasting of his arrest for the killing of Willie Robinson—and a prime candidate too for the killing of the Freemans, according to Goodrich—admitting that he was now awaiting trial for the murder of Lizzy Robinson. No wonder the impact on the spectators was so devastating and immediate. There had been no intimation of such a development because, for all he had to say to his friends in the press, Beers told them nothing about his impending case, and the Commonwealth, to protect Sarah Jane and himself from probable prejudice, had kept from the public the grand jury's decision to indict the pair of them for Lizzy's death.

Goodrich's cross-examination of Beers was so uncompromisingly direct that conflict between the two was inevitable. Counsel wanted exact answers and Beers's vagueness and belligerence annoyed him. Judge Field warned Beers several times about his conduct but the irrepressible witness refused to be deprived of his moment of fame. Goodrich's persistence eventually told, though, and by the end of his cross-examination Dr Beers was presented in a poor light; his memory was defective and his answers, given in a slapdash manner, were now reduced to "yes" or "no," with "sir" tacked on at the end, but very little else.

Beers was first forced to admit he was neither a dentist nor a doctor, but he still maintained he could practise medicine. In trying to explain this he managed only to enmesh himself and his listeners in a mass of irrelevancies. He lived mainly by the sale of a bottled mixture which, he claimed, cured alcoholism and drug-addiction. He compounded confusion then by adding the intriguing tit-bit that he could also "cure neuralgia by electric baths." Once again he denied giving medicine to the Freemans and rejected Goodrich's accusation that his interest in Mrs Robinson was motivated by his desire to get his hands on her insurance money. As Goodrich's questions became more pointed and provocative, Beers became more sullen and silent. When Goodrich had at last drained him dry, he dismissed him.

In spite of the defence's tough cross-questioning of Beers, what had it achieved? Not much. Although Beers's revelations had shocked the public and increased newspaper circulation, in terms of substantive evidence his contribution was trivial.

The two remaining days of the trial were taken up with counsels' closing arguments and Judge Knowlton's lengthy instruction to the jury.

John Goodrich's closing address followed the familiar formula. He told the jury that, where Mr Freeman's death was concerned, popular clamour and prejudice, prejudgement and common opinion, were all open to error and must be ignored. Sarah Jane, he instructed, was to be presumed innocent of all wrongdoings, notwithstanding coincidental deaths and the loose tongues of neighbours. Then, after warning the jury that solid evidence alone was all they could consider, Goodrich once more led them headlong through his maze of ingenious, though improbable, alternative interpretations. His most favoured explanation for Prince Arthur's death was natural causes, but his other grander theories, embracing the twin possibilities of death from inhalation of deadly fumes or from medicine given him by Beers, were again ventilated.

The jury must have seen through his tactics. Sarah Jane's lawyer made a far more telling point when he emphasised the Commonwealth's failure to connect—even remotely—his client with the possession of arsenic, the alleged means of death. Goodrich reasonably claimed that such a failure was powerful and decisive evidence in her favour, and on that fact alone they should find her not guilty. "A verdict which will at last deliver the prisoner at the bar after her long confinement from this terrible charge of an unnatural and monstrous crime."

Attorney-General Waterman had a different picture to paint. The case for the defence, he said, rested on rare possibilities, so rare, in fact, that they could be discounted with safety. Straight away he discarded as irrelevant the central thrust of Goodrich's contention that Freeman had died of natural causes, saying the available facts told against such a claim. And he attacked as nonsensical the defence assumptions concerning the seepage of arsenic through broken coffins and about death from poisonous fumes or from concoctions administered by Beers. Though hardly any more rational, he countered by insisting that the simplest and therefore the likeliest explanation was that the prisoner, whose compulsive desire for material comforts had been hampered by lack of finance, deliberately murdered the insured Freeman to secure the necessary funds.

Waterman maintained that the persuasive force of the medical and other testimony supported his view and was strong enough to bind the prisoner directly to the death of Prince Arthur Freeman. But should they still have doubts, such doubts must favour the accused, he told the jury.

Judge Knowlton commenced his charge to the jurors by advising them that the indictment itself was not to be considered as an indication of the prisoner's guilt. She was to be presumed innocent until proven guilty beyond doubt and *all* defendants were entitled to the benefit of that presumption. The judge then took the case asunder and examined the evidence piece by piece in a prolonged and impartial summing-up. He closed by directing the jury that they were not in court to ask the question, who murdered Mrs Freeman? Solving mysteries was no part of their function, he told them. The question they had to ask themselves was: did the accused kill her brother-in-law?

The jury thought she did, and found her guilty. She was sentenced to death, a decision upheld on appeal but later commuted to one of life imprisonment.

But Sarah Jane was responsible for more than the death of Prince Freeman. Two days after the result of William's post-mortem examination became known, men with shovels and exhumation orders descended on Mrs Robinson's plot in Garden Cemetery, Cambridge and dug up all her dead relatives. As evidence at her two trials had shown, arsenic was discovered in the remains of Willie, Annie and Prince. But what neither court had heard was the outcome of autopsies carried out on other family members. Moses, her husband, who had died in July 1882, Emma, her daughter, who had died in August 1884, and Lizzy, another daughter, who had died in February 1886, were all found to be saturated with arsenic. Then, for good measure—and no doubt to compensate for their earlier lack of interest in Sarah Jane's doings—the police exhumed the body of Oliver Sleeper, a one-time landlord of the Robinsons, and found that he, too, was permeated with poison. Although they were late arriving at the conclusion, the police were eventually absolutely certain that Sarah Jane was responsible for each and every one of their deaths. And, because of further evidence placed before it, the grand jury was also convinced, handing down four separate indictments against her, one each for the killing of Oliver Sleeper, Moses Robinson, Thomas Freeman and, with CC Beers, for the killing of Lizzy Robinson.

As a poisoner, she was certainly as improbable as any in the history of crime, but if ever a woman was miscast as a masterful murderer, it was Sarah Jane Robinson.

The press of America portrayed her as a fiendishly clever poisoner, full of subterfuge and careful planning. She was nothing of the sort; she violated all the established rules for murder. By their theory of evil conniving, the newspapers were bestowing on Sarah Jane a degree of subtlety she never displayed. Indeed, it seemed beyond the range of her intellect to understand the certain consequences of her actions, and the indiscriminate barbarity of her slaughter suggests she went into the business of wholesale murder undisturbed by any grasp of reality.

After killing her landlord, she devised no new techniques for the disposal of family members and made no plans for her own immunity from detection. In fact, her utter recklessness makes it appear she was indifferent to arrest. In the single-mindedness of her pursuit of victims, she became not only incautious but impetuous, showing as little respect for the mathematics of chance as she did for the family she poisoned. Her prophecies of their impending deaths she hollered from the rooftops, and with incredible stupidity she hounded insurance officials before and after funerals. Forever remote, she distanced herself from everyone and, according to several witnesses at her trial, rarely engaged in everyday chit-chat or gossip. Her one concession to sociability was to invite neighbours in to view her expensive furniture, which reveals the distorted importance she placed on the acquisition of household goods. The only other time she had callers was during family sicknesses, when she predicted deaths and spoke of her contact with the dead. It may be that in her tormented imagination she believed in her phantom visitors, until in the end they became a sort of self-fulfilling prophecy. That she believed them is one thing. But it now seems incomprehensible that, having left a trail a mile wide, her stumbling explanations about message-bearing spirits should have been taken seriously by anyone, when members of her family were dying around her like flies. And as she must have been perpetually living on the threshold of crises, it seems quite astonishing that her career of murder was not detected sooner. But Sarah Jane fumbled her way from one murder to the next with an incompetence matched only by the Boston police, who, like the Keystone Kops, wrote the script for their own farce as they tripped over the obvious.

Between her murder trials, which were two of the most widely publicised of the last century, everyone in America came to know Mrs Robinson. But only for a while; she soon became yesterday's news. Unlike Lizzy Borden, Sarah Jane made no lasting impression on American criminal history or its folklore. And unlike the public's reaction to Lizzy Borden, which changed radically, transforming her from murderer to martyr, no hysterical wave of sympathy swept America for Armagh's mass murderess. Sarah Jane and her systematic slaughter was a memory Americans wanted to forget, which they did as soon as she had been locked behind bars.

Although the question of her sanity had never been raised at her trial, medical experts who examined her in jail declared her to be mentally ill. No one who had watched her in court would have been surprised by the diagnosis. Typically, she continued to proclaim her innocence while remaining totally unmoved by the agonising deaths she had contrived for her eight victims. Unperturbed by her imprisonment, Sarah Jane Robinson lived to the age of sixty-seven. She died peacefully in her cell in 1906.

6

THE COOMBE COTTAGE MURDER

Charlotte Bryant   Dorset, England, 1936

When Frederick Bryant died in the Yeatman Hospital, Sherborne, Dorset, England, on 22 December 1935, the attendant doctor refused to issue a death certificate. Later, a post-mortem revealed the presence of arsenic in the remains, and seven weeks after his death Charlotte Bryant was charged with the murder of her husband. Her trial the following May provoked enormous interest, completely overshadowing all other criminal hearings in Britain during 1936, including the trials of seven other alleged murderesses. The magnetic ingredient which lifted the case above the ordinary—and made it a national sensation when spread over thousands of columns of newsprint—was the insatiable sexual appetite of the accused. Charlotte Bryant was a sensualist but far removed from the seductive sirens of Greek legend or the heroines of paperback romance. As journalists who were at the magistrates court reported, spectators were visibly shocked when seeing Mrs Bryant for the first time.

At thirty-three, her face was prematurely marked with the lines of despair and dissipation. Poverty and the birth of five children had also aged her before her time. She had just one tooth remaining in her mouth, and her hair, which had later to be de-loused by the prison authorities, hung in rats'-

tails from beneath her tight-fitting hat on her first morning in court. Her awful appearance must have prompted many to ask how such an unkempt woman could have aroused passion in the soul of any man. The answer, of course, was that Charlotte Bryant at one time had looked very different.

In 1921, as a vivacious teenager, Charlotte McHugh was understandably popular with the soldiers of the British army garrisoned in her home town of Derry in Ireland. The background of civil unrest and reprisals that was part of her young life did nothing to curtail her amorous and adventurous spirit, even though she was threatened, according to herself, with tarring and feathering by Home Rule militants for being too free with her favours in the barracks. She was born of gypsy stock, a fact that showed in her coal-black hair—her most distinctive feature—and the dark complexion of her skin, looks which helped, no doubt, to captivate Corporal Frederick Bryant, a twenty-five-year-old military policeman serving with the Dorset Regiment. Early the next year when Bryant was about to return home, the lovely Irish girl eloped with him to England. She was nineteen when they married at Wells in Somerset in March 1922. After several spells of casual employment, in 1925 Frederick Bryant took a permanent job as a herdsman and labourer at a farm at Over Compton, near Yeovil. The couple were given a cottage for the duration of Bryant's employment. The farm was in an out-of-the-way place with little to amuse or entertain Charlotte, the outgoing young woman who always enjoyed the bright lights and the company of young men. No doubt she saw her escape with Bryant from Derry's upheavals as an opportunity to find love and happiness but the hopes and dreams that she nurtured were not sustained because of the poverty and isolation of the narrow life she led in their four-roomed stone cottage. And her remoteness was not merely physical—Charlotte Bryant could neither read nor write. Had she been able to derive some fulfilment by reading, by identifying perhaps with glamorous or exciting heroines, or had she immersed herself in community affairs, she might have been happy and saved from the worst excesses of her troubled nature. But this is far from certain for Charlotte's lusting seems very close to nymphomania. One way or the other, her already drab existence was severely circumscribed by her illiteracy.

As far as Frederick Bryant was concerned, he seems to have been a quiet reserved type of man who kept very much to himself. Newspapers of the day have little to say about him, apart from reporting on his army career and describing the circumstances of his death. Of course, after his death, as with almost every victim of murder, Bryant was instantly dismissed from the minds of the press, while his alleged killer earned page after page of national exposure in the very same papers. What we do know of Bryant is that he was a man whose immense tolerance of his wife's lifestyle turned first to complacency and ultimately to complete indifference.

Neither he nor Charlotte was able to make the many necessary adjustments required in the transition to the married state and Charlotte was the first to realise the mistake she had made. She found nothing comforting in the routine of daily living and was soon in revolt against the restrictions of her new life. It was said that because of a leg-wound received in World War I Bryant was unable to satisfy his wife's sexual needs and that he allowed her to compensate for his inadequacy by associating with other men. If this was so, Charlotte took advantage of his complaisance.

Although the cottage offered few agreeable facilities for debauchery, Charlotte Bryant started her sexual exploits outside marriage by inducing local men into her bed while her husband was working about the farm. Most of her clients were as poor as herself and, while her desire was for excitement rather than money, they did occasionally pay a little for their pleasures, which supplemented Bryant's meagre wage of less than £2 a week. With increasing frequency, she strayed off at night to the village pubs, gratifying her need for immediate sexual satisfaction by disappearing down a lane with her current drinking partner. In time, her visits became a nightly ritual, her reputation deteriorating with each new scandalous adventure.

In December 1933, in the company of her husband, she met Leonard Parsons, the man who became the symbol of romance and the dominant obsession of her life. Parsons, who sometimes called himself Bill Moss, was, like herself, of gypsy origin. He was a travelling hawker and horse-dealer. He had Christmas dinner at their cottage and when he complained of his poor lodgings Bryant, with little discussion on the matter, invited him to stay with them as a paying guest. At night his bed was a couch in the parlour and in the morning he took Bryant's place beside Charlotte when her husband left for the farm, an arrangement that seems to have greatly pleased all three. And there is not the slightest doubt that Frederick Bryant knew of his wife's sluttish behaviour, for he told a complaining neighbour that he did not care what she did, adding that she was making twice as much money as he himself could earn in a week. But Bryant, who for years had accepted his wife's liaisons with complacency, finally had to take notice when his employer sacked him for turning his cottage into a bawdy house. Forced to find alternative accommodation, Bryant moved in the spring of 1934 to another tied cottage, this time at Coombe, a couple of miles from Sherborne, working once more as a farm labourer. It was probably too late then, but Bryant spurned any slight opportunity there might have been of regulating his wife's immoral habits, for when he installed Charlotte and the children in their new home, Leonard Parsons moved in with them.

Yet, however accommodating the timid Bryant was with his wife's behaviour, the potentially explosive situation clearly could not continue indefinitely—nor did it. When Charlotte's constant neglect of her duties allowed their home to slip from untidiness to filth and disorder, Bryant finally mustered enough gumption to tell Parsons to take himself off somewhere else. His wife was desolate at the thought of losing her lover. The intensity of Charlotte's passion for Parsons can be seen in its most extreme in her response to her husband's insistence that their lodger must leave. On the Saturday Parsons moved out, Charlotte collected two of her children, Billy and Lily, and went along with him. They travelled to Dorchester where they spent the weekend as a family, all sharing the same room. As she was always inclined to go her own way, Charlotte's sudden disappearance was not an event likely to worry Bryant, although he would have been concerned about his son and daughter. If he reasoned that Parsons would not take long to shed the burden of a married woman and two children, he was quite correct. On Monday evening when Bryant returned from the fields, he found his wife already at home preparing his supper. The explanation for her reappearance was that she had missed her other children, including the most recent, which had been fathered by Parsons. Needless to say, Bryant welcomed her back. Later in court, when it was suggested to her that a heated argument had followed her weekend excursion to Dorchester, Charlotte replied that not only had no such row taken place, but her husband had not even bothered to enquire where she had been. Perhaps she was telling the truth. That he realised questions were now irrelevant and that he no longer much cared what Charlotte did, was confirmed by the extraordinary happenings of the following week.

On the Thursday Leonard Parsons sent Charlotte a telegram, from an address in Babylon Hill, asking her to meet him at his new lodgings. When she asked her husband to read the message for her, Bryant declared they would both go to see Parsons and have a good talk with him. When they met, as Charlotte tried to keep the peace, Bryant and Parsons flung violent oaths and insults at each other, though no blows were actually exchanged. Eventually, with the calming influence of the woman of the triangle, husband and paramour became more reasoned in their discussions about her, and the upshot of this conference was that when Charlotte and Frederick returned to their cottage, they brought Leonard Parsons home with them. The peculiar solution arrived at would seem to suggest that, while the easy-going Bryant had no objection to his wife and their re-installed lodger continuing much as before, he put his foot down when it came to the pedlar taking Charlotte away altogether. It suggests something else as well which, in the light of later allegations, is of considerable significance. Frederick Bryant seemed every bit as taken with Parsons as Charlotte was. Except for the altercation at Babylon Hill, they were never known to be less than friendly towards each other. And Bryant, who at the best of times was a poor socialiser, often went drinking with Parsons, who seems to have been one of the few friends he had. Charlotte sometimes joined them to form a lively trio which did much to shock the local folk and bring more grist to the gossips' mill.

Because of his wandering occupation, Parsons was an irregular guest at the Coombe cottage, frequently staying away for days at a time to transact business on the south coast, usually at Plymouth and Weymouth. Occasionally Charlotte accompanied him as his wife on these hawking trips; still Bryant found no reason to quarrel with either of them on that account.

On the morning of 14 May 1935, Charlotte and her eldest boy, Ernest, went off with Parsons on one of those periodic day-trips, returning to Coombe between 8.00p.m. and 9.00p.m. that evening. While they were away, Frederick Bryant was violently sick. A neighbour who called at the Bryants' cottage about 3.00p.m. found Frederick crouched at the bottom of the stairs in obvious distress and complaining of terrible pains in his stomach. Bryant's neighbour did what she could to help but he was still shaking and suffering from cramp in his legs at 6.30p.m. when a local GP, Dr McCarthy, came to see him. The doctor diagnosed gastro-enteritis as the cause of the trouble. His patient improved enough to return to work on 18 May, four days later. The next time Frederick Bryant became ill, on 6 August, Dr McCarthy was not available to examine him, but Dr Mackintosh, his partner, answered the sick call and Bryant was again treated for gastro-enteritis. On 10 August, Bryant was up on his feet and once more went back to work.

After Frederick's second bout of illness, life in the Bryant household seems to have drifted along uneventfully until November, when Leonard Parsons's interest in Charlotte waned and he finally washed his hands of her. He told her there were better opportunities for trading elsewhere but it is more likely that he had tired of a mistress whose only remaining attraction was her availability; or he may simply have been drained from the sexual demands she made on him. Anyway, he ignored her fervent pleading and left Coombe at the end of the month, never returning to the cottage. In a fruitless gesture of frustration, before he left she hid his clothes, hoping no doubt that he would come back to collect them, and was depressed when her ploy failed. And days spent scouring the Dorset countryside as she called on Parsons's customers and cronies looking for information that would help her locate her lover were no more successful.

On 11 December, about a fortnight after Parsons's departure, Frederick Bryant had a recurrence of his stomach trouble. The attack was not as serious as before but it was severe enough to have a doctor summoned. Dr Tracey, who had not previously treated Bryant, learned from Charlotte that her husband was often afflicted with such pains. A diet was recommended for his condition and after two days Bryant was out of pain and thought to be recovering. Although Dr Tracey had given her no reason to think such a thing, Charlotte developed a sudden pessimism about the health of her husband, expressing the view that he probably did not have much longer to live. She confided to a friend that Bryant was not covered by insurance but she seemed cheered by the thought that the British army would give him a military funeral.

Charlotte Bryant was not the only woman discarded by Parsons, and on 16 December in her continuing search for him she met another reject, Mrs Priscilla Loveridge, when she travelled north by hired car to a gypsy camp near Weston-super-Mare. Mrs Loveridge, who had lived with Parsons for eleven years and borne him four children, sympathised with her visitor when explaining that he was not at the camp nor had he recently been there. Then, when she noticed the striking resemblance of Charlotte's child to Parsons, she quickly changed her tune and became threatening; her mother, Mrs Penfold, a colourful woman who smoked a pipe and cursed with wonderful fluency, became hysterical and abusive. After an uncomfortable twenty minutes, Charlotte, her journey a disaster, went home to Coombe in great despair. Why she brought the baby with her to the gypsy camp is not clear. She may have thought that if Parsons was there, the child might help to lure him from the camp and back to Coombe Cottage. Even had he been present, it is certain he was finished with Charlotte. In the end, all her visit achieved was to ensure the presence of her two tormentors as witnesses for the prosecution later at her trial.

Although distraught that all her efforts to trace Parsons had failed, Charlotte's mind was immediately occupied on her return with the arrival of an alternative guest at the cottage. This time the lodger was a woman. Mrs Lucy Ostler, a widow and friend of Charlotte, came with her seven children to keep her hostess company and share in the job of minding each other's youngsters. She slept at night in an armchair in the Bryants' bedroom. What Bryant thought of his wife's guests is not known but he was probably too weak to object even to the noise of twelve gallivanting children, because during the early hours of 21 December he once again became seriously ill. The following morning, despite his obstinate refusal to be moved, Dr McCarthy had him taken by ambulance to the Yeatman Hospital, Sherborne. At about 3.00p.m. on Sunday, 22 December, six hours after admission, Frederick Bryant died, confirming Charlotte's dire predictions.

Dr McCarthy considered that there were mysterious circumstances surrounding the death of his patient and reported his suspicions to the Sherborne police.

With the loss of her husband came the loss of her home, so Charlotte and her five children were shunted by the local health authority to the Sturminster Newton Institution, an old workhouse laid out in dormitories. On Monday she called to the hospital to collect her dead husband's clothes and to make arrangements to claim his body for burial. She was informed that a certificate of death could not be issued until such time as the result of an autopsy was known.

The post-mortem examination took place on 28 December. Dr Roche Lynch, Home Office analyst, reported to the police his discovery of four grams of arsenic in the corpse of Frederick Bryant.

Anticipating such a finding, the police had acted. In response to a request for assistance from the Chief Constable of Dorset, the London Metropolitan Police asked Chief Inspector Bell of Scotland Yard's Murder Squad to take charge of the case. He travelled to Sherborne with Detective Sergeant Tapsell. There, in conference with Superintendent Cherett of the local force, they arranged for the Bryants' cottage to be minutely examined for incriminating evidence. Working on twenty-one separate days over a period of seven weeks, a team of specialists almost took the cottage apart. Other officers were assigned the task of studying the gardens and surrounding countryside, the work done mostly on their hands and knees in wet or freezing conditions. In the squalid interior every corner, cupboard and container was searched. Floors, walls and chimneys were swept, and dirt, dust and soot were taken away for chemical and microscopic examination. An additional piece of evidence, a partly burnt and battered tin—which the prosecution would claim was of powerful significance—was discovered in a pile of household refuse in the yard. Of a total of almost

150 samples amassed by the police, traces of arsenic were found in thirty of them.

The police had two obvious suspects. At the time of his fatal illness Lucy Ostler and Charlotte Bryant were the only adults in close association with the victim. When detained and questioned, both women adamantly denied any knowledge of his death or the possession or purchase of any type of poison. Chief Inspector Bell was confident that he could disprove the claim of at least one of his suspects when he located a Yeovil pharmacist who said he clearly remembered selling a tin of arsenic-based weedkiller to a poorly dressed woman who signed the poison book with an X. The friends joined the line of an identification parade while the Yeovil chemist studied each member in turn. He failed to recognise the woman who bought the tin of weedkiller.

The failure to prove the suspected murderer's source or possession of poison left the police without presentable evidence, and in the ordinary way that might have been the end of the matter. But then a peculiar thing happened that put the case into the national headlines. The police suddenly discovered a witness who could help prove that Charlotte Bryant had poisoned her husband. And they did not have far to look; the vital witness was their other suspect, Lucy Ostler.

Mrs Ostler told the police that whilst she had been staying with the Bryants, Charlotte had spoken of the need to dispose of a tin which seemed to have a good deal of stuff in it. The tin was burned in the fire and later thrown out with the ashes. And, she said, she was present when Charlotte gave her husband a drink after which he became violently sick. On the strength of these and other allegations, the police took action. Shortly after sending three of her children to school, Charlotte was arrested on Monday, 10 February, at the Sturminster Newton Institution and charged with the murder of her husband. Two hours later she appeared before the Sherborne magistrates.

When it was opened to the public at 11.00a.m., the small Sherborne courtroom was quickly filled and an overflow audience of sensation-seekers jammed the entrance to the building and spilled out on to the street. Every major newspaper in Britain was represented at the hearing to bring news of a sultry adulteress to a nation of avid readers. But the reporters were stunned by the haggard appearance of the leading lady in the drama, who seemed as curious of the assembled press corps as they were of her. To the newsmen, she remained an enigma. After several adjournments, she was returned on 20 March to Exeter Prison to await her trial for murder. Some snippets of scandalous evidence heard at the lower court and rumours of further revelations to come guaranteed another packed courtroom when she made her next public appearance at Dorchester.

Mr Justice McKinnon presided at Charlotte Bryant's trial, which opened at the Dorset Assize Court in Dorchester on Wednesday, 27 May 1936. The Solicitor-General, Sir Terence O'Connor KC, led the team for the prosecution. The prisoner's defence was conducted by Mr JD Casswell. An air of unreality dominated the proceedings, with most of the witnesses and the accused seeming not to realise the seriousness of the occasion. Charlotte certainly underestimated the dangers posed by her trial and never foresaw the potential jeopardy of her predicament.

As Sir Terence O'Connor reconstructed events for the benefit of the jury in his opening presentation, he wisely skirted around the vital flaw in his own case—that no poison had been traced to Charlotte Bryant. Instead, he stressed her determination to rid herself of her husband so that she could live permanently and without interference with her gypsy lover, Leonard Parsons. And he promised he would bring forward witnesses who would prove to the jury's satisfaction that some of Charlotte's remarks and actions indicated that she, and she alone, was responsible for the criminal destruction of her husband, Frederick.

Parts of his statement really made no sense. The Solicitor-General's assertion that Charlotte murdered her husband so that she might entice Parsons back into her life was, at best, mere speculation. As evidence, it was worthless without supporting testimony, and none was presented in court. In building its case against her, the Crown produced more than thirty witnesses. Not one of them swore to knowing of even a hint of jealousy on Bryant's part as a result of his wife's extramarital exploits. During a five-month investigation—in which, it seems, anyone who ever met Charlotte and Frederick was questioned—the prosecution failed to present a single witness who had ever heard Bryant express the slightest annoyance or disapproval of his wife's illicit association with Parsons—or, for that matter, with anyone else. Later, Casswell reminded the jury of these facts and pointed out to them that Charlotte had no need to kill her husband, for he offered no obstacle or hindrance to her pursuit of men. Still, the idea of motive, as perceived by Sir Terence O'Connor, had been planted in the minds of the jury and it probably stayed there.

The prosecution placed its chief reliance on the evidence of Lucy Ostler. Mrs Ostler repeated the story she had earlier told the police, testimony that was highly damaging to her ex-friend Charlotte, who sat in the dock a few paces away from her. First she described what she heard when she woke in her chair in the Bryants' bedroom at about 3.00 a.m. on 21 December. Charlotte, she said, was encouraging her husband to finish a drink of *Oxo* which she held to his mouth. Moments later, Bryant vomited and began moaning as if he were in pain. After this disturbance Mrs Ostler dozed back to sleep and remembered nothing more of that night. Prompted by the Solicitor-General, she next related how Charlotte confessed to a hatred of her husband, and, in answer to the witness's enquiry why she did not leave him and go away with Parsons, Charlotte allegedly replied that she could not part from her children. Monday, 23 December, Mrs Ostler continued, was the day when her friend informed

SEAN O'BRIEN

her that she would have to dispose of a tin—a tin on which Mrs Ostler recognised the word *poison*—and went to the boiler, talking of setting fire to some rubbish. On another occasion when, in answer to a question by her friend, Mrs Ostler described an inquest as a sort of operation on a dead person, Charlotte answered that if the hospital "can't find anything, they can't put a rope around your neck." Finally, Lucy Ostler recalled for the Solicitor-General Charlotte's remarks about the likelihood of her husband's imminent death.

Mrs Ostler's evidence, though it was for the most part uncorroborated, still created damning implications that could not easily be explained away and, although defence counsel tried desperately to challenge her story, the job of questioning her must have been a disheartening prospect.

In cross-examination, Casswell put it to Mrs Ostler that she was friendly with the prisoner up to the time of their detention and changed her story only when the police viewed her part in the death of Frederick Bryant with as much suspicion as that which attached to the accused. The slur implicit in the question provoked her into angry retaliation. She declared hotly that there was no story to change and categorically denied any attempt to do so. But in a series of snappish answers Lucy Ostler admitted she was frightened when asked to take part in the identification parade. She was also forced to admit that, while helping to nurse Bryant in his final illness, she had more than once given him medicine. And she agreed reluctantly with Mr Casswell that she had as much opportunity as the prisoner to bring about the death of Frederick Bryant.

Although she was not at ease under defence counsel's questioning, often giving him ill-mannered or unresponsive replies, the most Casswell accomplished was to get Mrs Ostler to admit that she *could* have administered poison to the husband of the accused.

The Crown's suggested motive for Charlotte's killing Bryant was nonsensical but the defence's suggestion why

114

Mrs Ostler might have done so was non-existent.

Sir Terence O'Connor's address to the jury and Casswell's questioning of Lucy Ostler opened and closed the first day of the trial, with neither doing much to aid Charlotte Bryant.

On the second morning of the hearing, the Solicitor-General called Leonard Parsons to give evidence. The witness took up a very defensive stance from the moment he was sworn in. After identifying himself and stating his occupation, he was asked if he and Mrs Bryant had been intimate. Sir Terence received a surprising "No" to his query. The prosecutor, who did not regard this as an answer, reshaped his question several times before he eventually drew from Parsons the reply that they did have sexual intercourse regularly "from the time we met until the day I left." Even with careful handling, Sir Terence failed to prevent his own witness from looking awkward and foolish, but that, of course, did not stop Parsons from making many serious allegations against his former lover. He denied ever having weedkiller himself and that he ever brought weedkiller to Mr and Mrs Bryant's cottage, but he recalled some remarks he heard passing between the Bryants about just such a substance. On a day in August 1935, Parsons declared, Bryant was looking for his razor on a shelf in the kitchen when he asked his wife, "What's this?" and she answered, "That's weedkiller." He finished his examination by telling the Solicitor-General that Mrs Bryant suggested they should think about marriage as she was sure she would soon be a widow.

Mr Casswell wasted no time in letting the jury know what he thought of Leonard Parsons and his value as a witness. He asked rather acidly if the judge and jury were to take seriously the prosecution's claim that he was the kind of man Mrs Bryant would wish to marry, knowing he had no home to offer her and that he already had four illegitimate children whom he had deserted and failed to support. In what he evidently imagined was answer enough, Parsons replied that he and Mrs Bryant were on good terms. But Casswell hammered home the point that, as he had no regular occupation or apparent ambition beyond whoring and drinking, he was more a liability than an asset to Mrs Bryant or indeed to any woman. Then counsel stressed for the benefit of the jury the futility of relying on anything Parsons said when the witness admitted he had never seen the weedkiller referred to by the Bryants, as he was not in the kitchen at the time. When defence counsel asked the witness if the weedkiller could have been in a bottle or a cardboard box just as easily as in a tin, Parsons agreed that it could. Before he sat down, Casswell told Parsons he did not believe his story about his client's suggestion of marriage, nor, for that matter, did he believe one word of the witness's testimony. Leonard Parsons's accusations against his former Irish mistress were damaging but perhaps not as serious as they might have been, because of his poor showing under cross-examination. He was not a credible witness. Mr Justice McKinnon probably expressed the feelings of the majority of those in court when he afterwards told the jury in reference to Parsons, "I imagine you will regard him with the aversion he deserves."

A diversion from the grim reality of the trial was provided by the appearance of Priscilla Loveridge and her mother, Mrs Penfold. Both were dressed in outlandish clothes and covered in trinkets and baubles which created a noisy distraction whenever either of them moved. Priscilla— ignoring questions put to her by the Solicitor-General and later by Casswell—used her time in the limelight to castigate Parsons for deserting her and her children. She punctuated her evidence with vigorous gestures and grotesque facial contortions, and repeated every word of bad language which she had used when Charlotte called to the gypsy encampment in pursuit of Parsons. Only a tenuous order had been restored when Mrs Penfold entered the witness-box; she was even more cantankerous than her daughter, exhibiting an insolent hostility toward everyone in court, particularly Charlotte whom she threatened to choke, given the opportunity. She had an insuppressible urge to talk. Mr Justice McKinnon made several attempts to contain the witness but he could not get a word in edgeways.

The two women enlivened and confused the proceedings, certainly, but they offered very little in the way of substantive evidence. Sir Terence O'Connor claimed that their testimony clearly showed the prisoner's desperation to locate Parsons and her determination to get back with him at all costs. The implication was obvious: she was desperate enough to kill her husband to achieve her purpose. Even so, public opinion, which had been so strongly opposed to her before the trial opened, seemed at the end of the second day to shift a little in Charlotte's favour. Perhaps two days of hostile witnesses created a little sympathy for the drab figure in the dock. In the next two days feeling would swing again.

Of the prosecution's array of witnesses, by far the most impressive was Home Office senior analyst, Dr Gerald Roche Lynch, and his scientific evidence on the third day was thought to be the strongest element in the Crown's case.

The doctor told the jury that arsenic discovered in the remains of the victim amounted to four grams. Then, to support the contention that Frederick Bryant's death had resulted from a fatal dose of arsenic taken in an *Oxo* drink, he dissolved ten grams of weedkiller in a glass of warm water, together with an *Oxo* cube, and held aloft the stirred concoction for the jury's inspection. He told them there was no visible change of colour with the addition of the poison, and the jurors were content to take his word for it when he assured them that the taste of the mixture also remained unaltered.

Dealing with his examination of ashes taken from the cottage boiler-grate, Dr Roche Lynch said they contained 149 parts of arsenic per million, approximately three times the normal concentration found in domestic coal ash. This proportion indicated to him that some substance with a high arsenical content had been burnt in the fire. The weedkiller tin found with the house refuse was tested, he said, and this also contained traces of arsenic, as did several other samples of dust collected from the Bryants' cottage.

Dr Roche Lynch's evidence and his demonstrations from the witness-box were credible and dramatic. Taken with Mrs Ostler's earlier testimony of finding a burnt and misshapen tin in the grate of the boiler, they cannot have failed to impress the jury.

Other witnesses, whose evidence seems just as insubstantial and unimportant as any that had gone before, appeared on the last days of the trial. For instance, there was the farmer who had employed Bryant, a Mr Priddle. He told of having an argument with Charlotte about the hours she spent away from home and the little time she devoted to her sick husband. A Mr Tuck, an insurance agent, appeared to explain how he called to do business with Mrs Bryant on 20 December 1935 but would not have insured her husband because the man looked ill and seemed not to be a sound risk. When questioned by a very irate Casswell, this witness was forced into the admission that at no time was he asked to insure Frederick Bryant, nor had Mrs Bryant ever mentioned the possibility of seeking insurance cover for her husband. Still, the total effect of such evidence left Charlotte Bryant in a desperate situation when she stood in isolation to face the Solicitor-General on the final morning of the trial.

Charlotte proved to be an unexpectedly capable witness. She gave her evidence in a confident manner and her clear strong voice must have surprised many of her listeners. In spite of Sir Terence O'Connor's persistent questioning, she did not waver in any part of her story during her two hours' ordeal in the witness-box.

Mostly her testimony consisted of contradicting or denying statements made by witnesses for the prosecution. As far as her husband's last night of illness was concerned, she knew nothing, she said. That night she went to bed early, sleeping on undisturbed until breakfast time, when Ostler told her she had brought Bryant several drinks of water during the night. She told the prosecutor repeatedly that she had no knowledge of poison and obstinately refused to alter her evidence, even when shown the burnt weedkiller tin retrieved from her garden. Her husband might have had it in the cottage but she never saw it nor did she exchange any comments with him, she insisted, despite remarks attributed to her by Parsons. How was it then, the Solicitor-General wanted to know, that her evidence differed so fundamentally from the story told by so many of the Crown's witnesses? Had Parsons, Mrs Ostler and the others come to court simply to tell lies about her? Although she offered no real response to these questions and her own account of events lacked support from any source, observers at the trial maintained that she still managed to leave a favourable impression on those in court.

However impressive her performance, it is surprising she won much sympathy from her audience, for because of her unsavoury past her capacity to impress did not long survive the prosecutor's probing questions. It was common knowledge, of course, that her interest in men was not confined to her husband, but now emerged the sordid details of her life since her coming from Ireland. The jury heard how she initiated instant liaisons, had sex with strangers and neighbouring men alike, often in her husband's bed, and of her drinking bouts while her children were left at home unattended. In addition to these revelations, which for days formed the mainstay of conversation in Britain, Charlotte admitted to boasting vulgarly to acquaintances of her amorous conquests. She also agreed that she was well known as "Killarney Kate" and "Compton Liz". Disclosures of her sluttish life shocked the court yet, more than at her sexual gallivanting, the jury looked most disapproving when listening to evidence of the filthy condition of the cottage and of Charlotte's flagrant neglect of the children.

Tension in the courtroom was heightened when two of those children, ten-year-old Lucy and Ernest, aged twelve, followed their mother into the witness-box to give evidence in her defence. Because of Charlotte's loud weeping, several jurors sat forward to hear their words. Bowed heads and handkerchiefs told of the emotional response to the young witnesses by the court and at the moment of their appearance all sympathy for Charlotte evaporated. Nothing actually said by the children worsened her case but their very presence in the witness-box hardened hostility against Charlotte, creating the opposite effect to that hoped for by Casswell.

The closing speeches for both sides followed predictable lines. Sir Terence O'Connor said the prosecution case rested on two certainties. The disposal of the weedkiller tin by the accused implied an awareness of the outcome of the post-mortem, and poison in the body of Bryant could not have been administered inadvertently or innocently but was given callously and deliberately. He demanded a verdict of Guilty.

Defence counsel expressed disgust at the inclusion of many of the Crown's witnesses in the trial and ridiculed the bulk of their evidence as unbelievable fantasy. He produced no telling points in his client's favour but instead tried to implant in the minds of the jury apprehensions that they might convict an innocent woman. He told them she was not charged with neglect of her marital obligations but with murder.

In a rather short summing-up of the evidence, Mr Justice McKinnon told the jury to ask themselves two questions. Had Frederick Bryant died of arsenical poisoning?—a matter that was never in dispute—and, if they believed he had, did Charlotte Bryant administer that poison? The judge then pointed out that, although Parsons was staying at the cottage during Bryant's sicknesses of May and August and Mrs Ostler was present at the time of his final illness, only the prisoner was in attendance on every occasion. His summary could have given little comfort to the defence.

Just one hour after the case was submitted to them for consideration, the jury trooped back into court with the expected verdict of Guilty. Charlotte seemed unmoved by their decision. Not until the judge sentenced her to death did she react; the Derry woman who had failed to restrain her passion or her tongue, collapsed and was carried half-conscious to the cells beneath the dock.

The ink was hardly dry on the formal document of sentence when editors who had pursued Charlotte with the zeal of crusading moralists found that they had to change their tune radically. Quite suddenly Charlotte Bryant was the subject of a massive wave of public sympathy when most people came around to the opinion that, for the sake of the children, she should be spared. The press immediately launched an intensive campaign to save her from the scaffold, with readers participating in petitions and protests. Casswell's more sedate efforts to rescue her from impending death continued to the Court of Criminal Appeal.

Charlotte's counsel believed he had grounds for an appeal when he received a remarkable letter at his London home a few days after the trial's end. Having read a newspaper report of the case, Professor William Bone of the Imperial College of Science wrote to Casswell to say that Dr Roche Lynch had erred at the trial of Mrs Bryant when he gave evidence of the amounts of arsenic to be found in coal ash. While proportions differed with the various grades of coal, the professor claimed that the usual concentration was about 1000 parts of arsenic to the million. The quantity found in the ash taken from the Bryant grates was therefore exceedingly low, and not suspiciously high, as the Home Office analyst declared. The significance of this crucial information was not lost on Casswell, who realised that it tore to shreds the testimony of Mrs Lucy Ostler.

Neatly dressed in a blue suit and hat, Charlotte Bryant was in court to hear her counsel present her appeal on 29 June 1936. The Lord Chief Justice of England, Lord Hewart, with Mr Justice Finlay and Mr Justice Humphreys, was there to hear submissions. Charlotte's fate was virtually sealed from the beginning with the refusal of the Chief Justice to hear Professor Bone. Lord Hewart exclaimed petulantly that he found it objectionable to be expected to listen to scientific gentlemen expound theories about evidence they had not heard. He added that there was an abundance of other evidence to confirm the guilt of the appellant. The appeal was dismissed. Mr Casswell was shocked at the impatience of Lord Hewart and astonished by his remark that, "in this case it is clear there has been no mistake." What Justice Finlay or Justice Humphreys thought is not recorded. Neither spoke a word to the court.

It was not the business of the Court of Criminal Appeal to pronounce on the guilt or innocence of Charlotte Bryant. What the judges of the court had to determine was, if Professor Bone's additional evidence had been available and if they had been aware of the gross inaccuracies in the testimony of the Crown's scientific expert, would the jury at her trial have arrived at a different conclusion? His Lordship thought they would not. Charlotte's prosecutor, Sir Terence O'Connor, who told Casswell privately that "Lynch has certainly made a dreadful mistake," thought they would, and was in court to repeat his belief. But he, like Bone, was told by Lord Hewart that his presence was not required.

Back in the condemned cell, Charlotte agonised over her children. She desperately wanted to see Lily and Ernest to explain things to them but in her heart she knew they would never forget Dorchester and "...visiting me here would make things worse." In the end, to save them from further pain, she refused to see any of her family.

When not in prayer with her confessor, Father Barry, Charlotte spent her time in prison learning to read and write. Her new skills excited her and she progressed well enough to write several short notes, which made her very proud. To her son Ernest she wrote: "Think of me as I last was. I am thinking of you." As the date of her execution approached she addressed a message to the then uncrowned King Edward VIII claiming she was innocent and pleading, as a lowly and afflicted subject, "Don't let them kill me on Wednesday." When her plea for mercy was ignored, the last chance of a reprieve had gone.

Charlotte Bryant was thirty-three when her life was ended on the gallows of Exeter Prison on Wednesday, 15 July 1936. To the end she maintained her innocence. Four days later at the Church of the Sacred Heart, Father Barry advised his parishioners to shed no tears for Mrs Bryant, who had made her peace with God. He told them, "Her last moments were truly edifying."

Two days after she was hanged, her five children were taken into care by the Public Assistance Officer of the Dorset County Council.

At the time of her trial there were misgivings about the quality of much of the Crown's evidence and grave doubts were expressed about the justice of Charlotte's conviction and, later, about the dismissal of her appeal. Clearly, neither court satisfactorily resolved the contradictions presented by the bulk of ambiguous, misleading and uncorroborated evidence. Rather than giving an answer to the question, why did Charlotte poison her husband? the mass of uncertainties prompt the question, did Charlotte poison her husband? Doubts persist. Probably we will never know.

7

MURDER BY MARRIAGE

Dr Robert George Clements   Southport, England, 1947

The first the public learned of suspicions surrounding the death of Mrs Amy Victoria Clements was on 30 May 1947. While family and other mourners were assembling for her burial service in Southport, Lancashire, England, police arrived and stopped the funeral. They had acted on the direct instructions of their Chief Constable, Lt Col Harold Mighall. Dr Robert George Clements was not in church to hear that the body of the late Amy—the doctor's fourth wife—was to be removed to Southport Infirmary for a second post-mortem examination.

There was some early criticism of the authorities' intervention, but this quickly changed to accusations that the police had dallied indecisively when Dr Clements was found dead in his flat. He had taken his own life. Within days of his death, details of Dr Clements's life had become public property, causing a major sensation in Britain.

Robert George Clements was born in Limerick in 1880, where he attended local schools before going to Belfast in 1899 to study medicine. Soon after qualifying from Queen's University in 1906, he met Edyth Anna Mercier, the forty-year-old daughter of a wealthy grain merchant. The couple married in 1912, the year the doctor was admitted to the Royal College of Surgeons. Before the end of the year, Edyth inherited £25 000 on the death of her father.

The Clementses were well known in Belfast for their constant socialising and lavish entertaining, and Clements himself was easily recognised by his dandified clothes and extravagant tastes. He seemed to cultivate this image and had a theatrical fondness for the part, because he was rarely seen without top hat, cravat, chamois gloves, spats and a silver-mounted walking-stick, often at odd hours of the day or night. Men usually found the doctor pompous and overly polite but he was very popular with women, who comprised most of the patients in his practice, conducted from his surgery in the fashionable College Gardens.

Then in 1920, at a time when he was well established and successful, Dr Clements became a widower for the first time. Following a short illness, Edyth died unexpectedly, of sleeping sickness, according to Clements, who signed his wife's death certificate.

Dr Clements moved to England but wrote often to a young woman friend in Belfast. Their passion by post progressed with such speed that when he set up a new practice in Manchester in 1921 he had a new wife to go with it. At twenty-one, and nearly as many years the doctor's junior, Mary McCleery, the daughter of another well-to-do Irish family, became the second Mrs Clements. She enjoyed the privilege for only four years. Her death in 1925 was attributed by her husband to endocarditis, and he furnished a death certificate to that effect.

When Edyth died in 1920, Clements had sought refuge in a change of location and moved to Manchester. Now, with the death of Mary, he decided to move again. This time he joined a shipping company and for a couple of years travelled in the Far East as a ship's surgeon, before returning at the end of 1927 to re-establish his practice in Manchester.

In 1928, the doctor decided to marry again. The third woman to take Clements's name in marriage was Kathleen Sarah Burke. She, too, was Irish but, unlike her deceased predecessors, she brought no money to the partnership. She and her husband appeared to be a happy stay-at-home couple who seldom entertained and were rarely seen together in public. With his earlier spouses Clements had lived an often hectic life but with his new wife he seemed to have led a quiet existence, with few signs of his former flamboyance. But there were occasional eccentric flourishes. One of these was the employment of a Japanese as butler. He doubled as receptionist, greeting patients with excessive courtesy, robed in an elaborate costume of Oriental splendour. He became a popular attraction for the curious and perfectly healthy Mancunians called at the surgery just to gape at him.

To his friends and colleagues alike, the next notable event in the doctor's life was every bit as odd and just as surprising. Still only fifty-three, and highly regarded in his profession, Dr Clements closed his practice in 1933, retired with Kathleen to Bournemouth on England's south coast and bought a small hotel which they managed together. (If the Japanese travelled with them, the fact went unrecorded.) But the couple's career as hoteliers was brief. Because Kathleen had never felt at home in the south, they sold the business in 1935 and returned to Lancashire, settling in Southport, where he was employed as senior physician at the Kenworthy Hydro.

It was in this Southport clinic that Dr Clements's misfortunes in marriage emerged for the third time, with the death of Kathleen in 1939. Cancer of the stomach was described as the cause of death on the certificate, signed, once again, by Dr Clements himself.

Later it would be claimed that Dr Clements's first two wives had died under peculiar circumstances. Perhaps they had but, however they met their ends, no doubts were expressed at the time of Edyth's death in Belfast, nor was there any public notice taken when Mary, the second Mrs Clements, died in Manchester. As far as anyone knew, the doctor's marriages had been happy ones, with the partners on good terms with each other. In other words, he was under no suspicion; all that changed when Kathleen died.

As had been the case on the two earlier occasions, Clements was again the only doctor to attend his wife in her final illness, and beyond his own statement that Kathleen had died of cancer of the stomach there was no evidence to support such a claim. There were at least two people who doubted the truth of it. The first, an anonymous informant, who purported to have been a neighbour of the dead woman, suggested to the police that someone should look into the death of the third Mrs Clements. The police rejected the advice, dismissing the letter as the work of a troublemaking crank. But they paid more attention to Dr Irene Gayus.

A shareholder in the Kenworthy Hydro, Dr Gayus had known both the Clementses, becoming a close friend of Kathleen, while developing an intense loathing of the doctor. She had never liked Clements, considering him egotistical with grandiose ideas about his social standing and professional ability. The discovery of his flirtations with women patients at the clinic, while he neglected his sick wife, angered and disgusted her. But, more significantly, with Kathleen's death, she began to be suspicious as well. Although Dr Gayus did not know precisely how Kathleen Clements had died, she was convinced it had nothing to do with stomach cancer. Only days earlier, she had seen her friend eat a large meal, an impossible task, she believed, for someone in the final stages of the disease. For a while Dr Gayus hesitated to express her suspicions, wondering if her enmity towards Dr Clements was distorting her professional judgement. Doubts persisted and eventually the nagging anxiety of it all led her to speak to Southport's Chief Constable.

As a result of his interview with Dr Gayus, Harold Mighall contacted the coroner, who agreed they needed answers to some disturbing questions. But there was a more immediate problem. They needed to halt the funeral of Mrs Clements. Liverpool CID was notified but, when officers rushed to Liverpool crematorium to claim the body for a post-mortem examination, they found it had already been cremated. So, before the police could investigate any possible involvement by Dr Clements in the death of his third wife, they were deprived of her corpse. However incriminating Dr Gayus's story, it was legally inconclusive and any real evidence that might have existed had been turned to ashes by the alleged victim's cremation. With no sure idea of how she had died, the authorities were powerless to act. Still, the police got busy tracing Dr Clements's background. They naturally concentrated their initial enquiries on Clements's relationship with his last wife—later they would explore his earlier marriages—but all they discovered was that the doctor spent money freely and was something of a dandy who enjoyed the company of women. Even so, the whole episode served to draw attention to him. The police were suspicious and would remain that way.

In the meantime, Dr Clements, who seemed not at all disconcerted or embarrassed by rumours concerning the death of his third wife, remained tranquil through his tribulations. Nor was it possible to dampen his ardour, for he lost no time in exerting his powerful Irish charm on his newest romantic interest. He did not have far to search to find her. Vivacious wealthy socialite, forty-year-old Amy Victoria Burnett, was one of Dr Clements's own patients. The doctor was also treating her father, a prosperous Liverpool industrialist, who died suddenly in January 1940, leaving his daughter £22 000 as her share of his estate. Six months later, at St George's church in Hanover Square, London, Amy Burnett became Mrs Clements the fourth, in one of the "society" weddings of the year, highlighted by a celebratory banquet, musically accompanied, for some 200 guests at the Savoy Hotel.

It was a memorable occasion; Amy's inheritance saw to that. The honeymooners stayed on to savour a week of metropolitan delights before returning to make their home in Amy's flat on Southport Promenade.

The newly-weds quickly immersed themselves in civic

and social activities. They both did charitable work for their church. Clements, now sixty, involved himself in Conservative politics; Amy, an accomplished pianist and composer, performed in musical productions to aid the war effort. She remained socially active up to the war's end; then, withdrawing from Southport society, she became a recluse.

There were bound to be questions asked as to why so vibrant a woman would shut herself away in her home, becoming so self-effacing as to be invisible and ending almost all contact with the outside world. Her husband, now Assistant Medical Officer of Health for Blackburn, had ready answers. The doctor explained to friends that his wife was having dizzy spells, recurring headaches and frequent lapses of memory, caused, he was sorry to tell them, by advancing mycloid leukaemia. It was odd, then, that when Dr John Holmes of Southport Infirmary was called in by Clements to examine Amy in December 1946, he discovered no evidence of disease of any description. But the next time Dr Holmes was sent for to attend to Mrs Clements, at 11.30 on the night of 26 May 1947, he found her unconscious and close to death. He had her transferred by ambulance to the Astley Bank nursing home, where he examined her in the company of Dr Andrew Brown, medical superintendent of the home, and Mrs Baxendale, its matron. They could do nothing for her. Mrs Clements never regained consciousness and died at 9.30 the following morning.

At that time, the two doctors were puzzled. Mrs Clements's skin had taken on a yellowish tint and both Dr Holmes and Dr Brown were disturbed by the contraction of the eye pupils, a recognised symptom of morphine overdose. It seemed to them possible that Amy Clements had been poisoned and had not died of leukaemia as stated by her husband. Unhappy with the seeming irregularities, Dr Holmes informed Clements that he could not issue a certificate in respect of his wife until a post-mortem examination had been carried out. Dr Clements could not have been more cooperative, agreeing that the cause of death should be determined. Then, without regard to established medical practice or legal requirements, he made immediate arrangements with a friend, pathologist Dr James Houston, to perform an autopsy.

Dr Houston, a young Irishman and, like Clements, a graduate of Queen's University, did not consider it necessary to complete a full chemical and microscopic examination. The reasons for his decision are unknown. Perhaps he was unduly influenced by Clements's suggestion that his wife's death was due to leukaemia. Whatever the reason, when he had conducted some blood tests and examined organs removed from the body—which were afterwards destroyed in an incinerator—he confirmed that mycloid leukaemia was indeed the cause of Mrs Clements's death. Dr Holmes, now satisfied, signed the certificate accordingly. Dr Brown was far from certain.

Dr Clements had now outlived four wives. Before the last of them could be finally put to rest, the intervening days would include a dramatic second autopsy on her body, the tragic suicide of Dr Houston, the man who had performed the first one, and the equally shocking suicide of Dr Clements, triggered by the persistent suspicions of Dr Andrew Brown. Despite James Houston's assertion that Mrs Clements had died of leukaemia, Dr Brown thought there may have been contributory causes and he was still troubled that *all* the details of her death had not been revealed. He went to the coroner and told him so. When Mr Cornelius Bottom, the West Lancashire coroner, heard from Dr Brown that both he and Dr Holmes had observed what they considered a suspicious complex of symptoms, including those consistent with morphine poisoning, he immediately contacted Lt Col Harold Mighall. This piece of information alarmed the chief constable. From his last experience of a dead Mrs Clements, he realised the need for speed and acted instantly. To try to establish for himself the exact details of how Amy Clements had died, he made two immediate calls before

deciding what further action to take. First he met with Dr
Houston, who told him he was quite sure that leukaemia
had been the cause of the woman's death, though he
admitted he had not examined the body for drugs. Then
Mighall went to see Dr Clements, who seemed remarkably
self-possessed. The doctor scoffed at the suggestion that
there was anything mysterious about his wife's death, and
said he was in complete agreement with Dr Houston's
findings, adding, "There is no known cure for leukaemia."

Far from satisfied with the results of these interviews,
Mighall ordered a full-scale enquiry into the circumstances
surrounding the death. There was now extreme pressure on
the chief constable, because preliminary arrangements for
Amy Clements's funeral had already been made.

In the first hours of their investigation, the Southport
police were given conflicting reports by those who knew the
doctor and his wife. Some sources—the majority—said they
were an affectionate pair who got on well together, with an
absence of even the mildest disputes. Others suggested
differently. For instance, Mary O'Keeffe, housekeeper to the
tenants of the ground-floor flat, had a curious story to tell.
She said that Mrs Clements had spoken to her occasionally
about her illness, complaining of bouts of vomiting, of a
loss of appetite and sleep, which often left her too weak to
do housework and so faint that she sometimes drifted into
unconsciousness. Still, she considered herself lucky,
explaining that Dr Clements always seemed to know a day
in advance when these attacks were about to happen and
would warn her to stay in bed. Miss O'Keeffe also told the
police that from time to time she had heard raised voices
overhead which sounded to her as if Dr Clements was angry
with his wife.

Another surprising report came from a Mrs Jean
McLachlan, who occupied a flat in the same building as the
Clementses. She informed detectives that, although the
doctor had told her his wife would not live much longer, she
was still very shocked by her death. As she had not seen the

reclusive Mrs Clements out of doors for months, it struck her as particularly odd when she noticed her entering the driveway to the house on the arm of her husband, laughing and seemingly in the best of health, at about 10.15 on the night before she died. There were a couple of things about this story that bothered the police. If Amy Clements was as seriously ill as the doctor maintained, how did she suddenly find the strength to go walking, and, if she was that strong at 10.15, why was she weak, senseless and dying at 11.30, when Dr Holmes was called to her bedside?

In addition to those people who had been visited by CID officers, the almost frantic nature of the investigation brought forward other witnesses who volunteered information to the police. Among them was Ursula Clarenden. Mrs Clarenden, a long-standing friend of Amy Clements, complained to the police that for some months previously Dr Clements had prevented her visiting his wife, saying she was far too ill to see anyone. She still kept in contact by ringing her friend a couple of times a week but this practice soon stopped when Dr Clements had the telephone disconnected.

The investigation had only moved into its second day but already the accumulating evidence convinced the chief constable that he should wait no longer. He ordered the postponement of Mrs Clements's funeral, and senior officers were sent to inform both Dr Clements and Dr Houston that there was going to be a second autopsy. Dr Houston, shocked when told of this development, replied, "I wish I had known about this before."

Officers who called on Dr Clements found him dead in his kitchen. After the chief constable's talk with him, life for the doctor must have become an ordeal of nerves. Perhaps he had a premonition of doom; anyway, faced with the possibility, if not the certainty, of a murder charge being brought against him, he chose to kill himself with an overdose of morphine. He left a suicide note which read, in part, "I can no longer stand this diabolical insult to me."

If Dr Houston's post-mortem examination had been of the hit-and-miss variety, Amy Clements's body was now subjected to detailed medical scrutiny in the second autopsy, conducted this time by Home Office pathologist, Dr WH Grace. Dr Grace did not have much to work with, though, because Dr Houston, after completing *his* tests, had instructed a morgue technician to burn the body's organs. Although aware of the problem, it was still a disappointment to the waiting police to learn that the pathologist had failed to discover the cause of death. Of course, this did nothing to dispel suspicions that Clements had murdered his wife. And, even if indecisive, Dr Grace's autopsy did produce one positive result; whatever it was that had killed Amy Clements, it was not leukaemia. Not a trace of the disease was found in the body.

Tragedy was to follow this revelation. Depressed by the news and appalled by the realisation that he had badly handled the original examination, Dr Houston went to his laboratory at Southport Infirmary and poisoned himself with a massive overdose of cyanide. He, too, left a suicide note. It ended: "I have for some time been aware that I was making mistakes. I have not profited by experience."

All over the country, newspapers reported Mrs Clements's death and some hinted at a much bigger story to come. Readers impatient for new disclosures did not have long to wait. The official announcement of Dr Clements's tragic suicide soon followed, and fascination with the enquiry grew stronger. But it was not until 2 June, when Dr Houston ended his life with such startling suddenness, that a vast army of journalists descended on Southport, determined in one way or another to satisfy the British public's curiosity.

Unfortunately, the investigation into the three deaths was conducted in a glare of sensational and often inaccurate reporting, with the police in a race to get witnesses' stories before the newspapermen. There were questioners everywhere, and if any witness in Southport was overlooked by either side in its search for information, he or she was indeed unique.

While the majority of journalists respected the occasional police request to withhold some sensitive item of news, others ignored the plea. Naturally, most published accounts accorded with the established facts but many of them did not. Statements that were sometimes contradictory, though attributed to the same source, created problems for the police and confusion in the minds of the public. Some newspapers implied that Dr Clements had probably murdered several wives, and there were suggestions that a deliberate conspiracy to conceal the truth was the reason for Dr Houston's failure to disclose the real cause of Mrs Clements's death. There were threats of legal suits being brought to restrain certain publications and, though no criminal prosecutions followed, the press would later be publicly censured for what was seen as its unethical handling of the whole Clements affair. Since it was in their respective interests, they did compare and exchange information but, with neither entirely trusting of the other, it was an uneasy alliance that existed between the invading press and the Southport police. For the nation's readers, it all added to the general excitement, though some of the dramatic effect of the Clements case was dulled for the public by the authorities' unwillingness to exhume the bodies of the doctor's first two wives. But, with three corpses already on their hands, official reluctance to dig up another two was understandable. As Clements was dead, the police said nothing could be gained by such action. Their decision refuelled gossip and revived rumours as the investigation continued.

When Dr Grace's autopsy report left the mystery of Amy Clements's death as much a mystery as ever, the police turned for help to one of Britain's foremost scientists, Dr JB Firth, director of the Home Office Forensic Science Laboratory at Preston. The authorities believed that if anyone could prove Dr Clements had murdered his wife, Dr Firth was the man to do it. And they were right.

Dr Firth accompanied detectives to Clements's flat,

where he found hundreds of medicine bottles and dozens of tubes and boxes of tablets. In one small bottle he discovered three three-quarters-of-a-grain morphine sodium tablets. When police checked the label reference-number, they found the original prescription had been for sleeping tablets. So someone had tampered with the bottle, replacing phenobarbitone tablets with morphine tablets. Who else but Dr Clements would have done that?

Even as it was, the police were fairly sure of Clements's guilt, but with their next important discoveries they were absolutely certain of it. On renewed visits to the flat, Dr Firth isolated several more bottles containing morphine tablets varying in strength between one-sixth and three-quarters of a grain. Local pharmacists' records soon revealed the sinister information that they had been prescribed for several of Clements's patients who had no need for such tablets and who had obviously never received them. Yet, in spite of that incriminating evidence, the police were no nearer than before to solving the real puzzle. And it began to appear that they never would, because both Dr Firth and the police were faced with the same problem—neither could actually *prove* that Dr Clements had poisoned his wife.

For Dr Firth and his colleagues back at the forensic laboratory in Preston, the task was far from simple, but their persistent efforts did end with spectacular results. It took them more than two weeks of exhaustive tests before they produced irrefutable proof that Clements had indeed deliberately killed his wife.

From the evidence already available, Dr Firth was confident he knew how Mrs Clements had lived out the last six months of her life. He also thought he could account for her death, though here he was merely guessing. As Dr Firth saw it, a steady supply of morphine tablets, given in the guise of harmless sleeping tablets by Dr Clements, had turned his wife into a drug addict, with symptoms which might be mistaken for those of natural disease. Then, on the night of 26 May, he ended her life with a fatal dose of morphine, probably administered by injection.

It was this piece of reasoned guesswork that would finally solve the case.

Dr Firth went back to Amy Clements's body and eventually found near the spine what he was looking for: the mark of a recent injection. As well as that small section of spine, he also brought to Preston a small amount of kidney. After long analysis, the scientist extracted from the kidney 1.34 milligrams of morphine and from the spine 0.8 milligrams of morphine, the remains of a much larger dose.

Allowing for the very small proportion of the body represented by the section of spine—it weighed under one ounce—Dr Firth disclosed that the amount of morphine discovered there indicated the injection would have been deadly.

Relieved, though not much surprised, the police at last had what they wanted. They had confirmed what they had long believed: Dr Clements was a murderer. Could they prove it—and would a coroner's jury agree with them?

The inquest on Mrs Clements, Dr Clements and Dr Houston, from which hundreds of would-be spectators had to be turned away, opened on 25 June before the coroner, Mr Bottom, and jury. It lasted three days. Within a matter of minutes, and before he had even outlined the history of events or called a single witness, the coroner started proceedings with a blistering criticism of the press. According to him, the irresponsible behaviour of some newspapers had clearly shown their cynical disregard for both the public interest and the principles of justice. When news was not forthcoming, they invented their own; with the absence of reliable information, wild rumour and dangerous gossip had taken its place. They had hampered the police, interfered with witnesses, in some instances buying snippets of news from strangers who claimed to be friends of the Clementses or Houstons, and published their remarks unchecked. Then, looking directly at the press benches, Bottom said that those who had disgraced their profession—and everybody knew who they were—could consider themselves fortunate not to be facing criminal charges. This lambasting of the press was followed by the customary injunction to a jury that really asked the impossible. The coroner said he wanted them to put out of their minds every word they had heard or read about the three deaths under review, to prevent prejudice from colouring their views and to base their verdict solely on the evidence that was to be placed before them. After a month of saturation coverage, it was asking a lot of any jury.

Mary O'Keeffe, Mrs McLachlan, Mrs Clarenden, and other friends and neighbours appeared before the inquest to repeat the stories told earlier to Southport detectives, evidence that clearly contradicted Dr Clements's explanation of his wife's illness. Police evidence included extracts from a diary of Dr Clements, in which tributes to his wife's fine qualities were unrestrained: "adorable wife"; "she was too good and devoted"; "never fair to herself." They also contained details of her worsening condition, attributing it to leukaemia. Dr Grace then told the jury that Mrs Clements had not died of leukaemia, while Dr Firth told them what she had died of—a lethal injection of morphine. In answer to questions put to him by the coroner, Dr Firth thought suicide could be discounted, as the location of the needle-mark almost certainly precluded the possibility of self-administration.

As Dr Clements was not available to defend his actions, Bottom warned the jury to be especially careful before judging for themselves whether the doctor had taken his own life while his mind was disturbed or had done so because he had murdered his wife and had foreseen his impending exposure.

Mrs Houston made a brief appearance at the inquest, telling the jury of the severe depression suffered for months by her late husband. She thought it had been brought on by an exceptionally heavy workload. So concerned was she by his condition, she contacted his parents in Ireland, suggesting a holiday there might improve his health. Referring to Dr Houston's post-mortem examination of Mrs Clements, Dr Cronin Lowe, pathologist to Southport Infirmary, said that, in his opinion, Dr Houston's diagnosis of leukaemia "was honest and genuine, but formed on insufficient evidence." Here again, Bottom advised the jury to exercise great care before making a decision on Dr Houston's death.

On the late afternoon of Thursday, 27 June 1947, the jury announced its verdicts: Amy Victoria Clements: murdered by her husband; Dr Robert George Clements: committed *felo-de-se* (self-murder); Dr James Montagu Houston: committed suicide while the balance of his mind was disturbed. The coroner thanked the police, the medical experts and all the other witnesses who had appeared before him. He thanked the jury too, telling them he was certain their verdicts were correct.

The inquest was over and the investigation officially closed on Clements but still there were doubts that the mystery was solved. With the jury hearing evidence on the death of just one Mrs Clements, it could hardly have been otherwise. Neither the jury's verdict nor the coroner's endorsement of it convinced many people that Clements had killed only one of his wives. The more charitable in their judgement claimed Clements was insane but the general public, wholly unsympathetic, saw Dr Clements as a systematic poisoner of four wives, his murderous career distinguished only by remorseless regularity. In Southport, nobody was sure as to why Clements poisoned four wives but everyone agreed that he had. The police shared the view that the doctor was up to his elbows in murder and it was only an improbable run of good fortune that delayed his exposure. They also knew why. Money was central to his enterprise, with his get-rich-quick schemes requiring nothing less than the premeditated murder of each wife. So entrenched was this opinion that it would have been hard to find a policeman in Belfast, Manchester or Southport to oppose it. But, irrespective of whose opinion it was, it was not evidence, nor was it a very comfortable explanation.

In the first place, the belief that Clements murdered his first two wives is not even remotely supported by facts. Then, although it is hard to resist the conclusion that Kathleen was done away with, even here there is a gaping hole in the police theory of murder for money. Kathleen, a Belfast shop-assistant, was penniless when she married Clements. Finally, what provoked immense interest at the time but remained unexplained, was Clements's *motive* for murdering his last wife. True, when she died, Amy Clements left £51 000 but Clements himself had more than £12 000 in his own account. So, in this instance, money would seem to have been an unlikely reason for murder. Mary O'Keeffe did tell the police of probable arguments between the doctor and his wife but there seems to be no reliable evidence that this was so. Anyway, murder, surely, would be an extreme antidote to such domestic troubles.

So it remains a mystery. No motive for the murder of Amy Clements seemed to exist. A coroner's jury did find her husband guilty of her killing, and because of his suicide, of course, Clements was never put to the embarrassment of having to explain her death. That is all that is known and it is unlikely that anyone will ever know more.

8

MURDER IN DISGUISE

Frederick Emmett-Dunne   Duisburg, Germany, 1955

The interest of this case, which took place in Germany, rests mainly on the unique method of killing employed by the murderer, a British army sergeant, and his elaborate efforts to conceal the crime, making it appear that the victim had taken his own life. For a while, the deception was successful.

Following a post-mortem examination by army pathologist, Dr Alan Womack, and a military court of enquiry, the death of Sergeant Reginald Walters, Royal Electrical and Mechanical Engineers, in Duisburg, Germany, on 30 November 1953, was recorded as suicide by hanging. The sergeant was buried in the British Military Cemetery, Cologne, and, as far as the army was concerned, the sad business of Reginald Walters was closed. But fourteen months later, in February 1954, after much bad-natured gossip, local suspicion and a further army enquiry, the body was disinterred and subjected to a second autopsy, conducted on this occasion by British Home Office pathologist, Dr Francis Camps. Camps found that the sergeant had died of a blow to the front of the throat which produced injuries not consistent with the original finding of Dr Womack.

The exhumation of Sergeant Walters's remains had taken place primarily as a result of the action of Assistant Provost-Marshal Frank Elliott, a member of the staff of the

Special Investigation Department of the British army. Elliott had been away from the regiment at the time of Walters's death. On his return, he was shocked to learn of the sergeant's suicide. Elliott had been friendly with Walters and had always known him to be carefree, cheerful and the driving force at any party. Nothing that was said of him suggested Walters would kill himself and Elliott could find few, in or out of the barracks, who believed the sergeant had taken his own life. He was also surprised at widespread stories going the rounds of the camp concerning the carry-on of the late sergeant's wife with another serviceman in the same regiment.

The SID man thought a re-checking of all the facts surrounding the sergeant's death was essential to dispel gossip and, if possible, disprove the rumours. One way or the other, when it became known in Duisburg that Mrs Walters had hastily remarried in England, the order for a full-scale investigation of her husband's last hours was only a matter of time. The army investigator communicated his suspicions to his superiors; then, in response to a request made to the Metropolitan Police in London, New Scotland Yard lent Detective Superintendent Colin McDougal to the army for the duration of the enquiry.

News that the superintendent was considering the exhumation of the dead sergeant brought a most unexpected reaction from an ex-army private living in England.

Ronald Emmett read a newspaper report of the marriage of Walters's widow, Maria, to his half-brother Frederick Emmett-Dunne on 3 June 1954—just seven months after Walters's death—and, although he gave the matter a good deal of thought, he said, he saw nothing at all sinister in the event. Later, seeing a press release of February 1955 that the police in Duisburg were going to dig up the body of Sergeant Walters, he changed his mind on the subject and walked into a police station in Hoylake, Cheshire, telling a story that was to make headlines in the nation's newspapers within days.

He was hesitant at first, saying only that he was not responsible for anything that had happened to Sergeant Walters. Then he admitted that he knew something of the death of the sergeant in Germany. After a little prodding and encouragement by the police, Emmett finally divulged the information he had called to give them.

He had helped his half-brother, he said, to lift up the already dead body of Sergeant Walters so that a noose could be tied around the neck and the body suspended to make it look like suicide. He later made a full written statement of his involvement in the charade.

Ronald Emmett's confession to the Hoylake police was transmitted to the army authorities in Germany with a request for instructions. It resulted in the arrest in Taunton, Somerset, of Frederick Emmett-Dunne, who was charged with the murder of Sergeant Reginald Walters.

When Emmett-Dunne faced the preliminary hearing of the charge at Bow Street Magistrates Court, London, there was an immediate dramatic development. His counsel said that Emmett-Dunne had been born in Dublin and the alleged murder had occurred in Germany, therefore an English court had no judicial function to perform in the matter. The present tribunal, he submitted, could not try an Irish citizen for a crime supposedly committed in a foreign land. After some deliberation the court agreed that the counsel's submissions were proper in law and dismissed the case against the prisoner, to the astonishment of the assembled newspapermen.

But Emmett-Dunne did not go free as a consequence of the court's judgement. He was taken in charge by members of the Royal Military Police and flown to an army detention centre in Bielefeld, Germany. There the charge was the same as that which he had faced in England—the murder of Sergeant Walters.

Frederick Emmett-Dunne's trial before a British military court martial, comprised of seven officers, opened on 27 June 1955, in Steel House, Düsseldorf, Germany. The president of the court was Brigadier DL Betts. Also in court, to give guidance on matters of law, was the judge-advocate, Mr C Cahn. Leading the prosecution team was civilian barrister, Mr Mervyn Griffith-Jones, while the accused was defended by another outside lawyer, Mr Curtis-Bennett QC. The last man to enter before the courtroom was sealed was Emmett-Dunne, a tall, powerful thirty-three-year-old, prematurely grey. With his uniform adorned with a chestful of medals, he looked what he was, a professional soldier.

Emmett-Dunne's record as a soldier was as impressive as his appearance. He was born in Dublin in 1922 and spent the first seventeen years of his life in that city. In 1939 he left Ireland to join the British army, enlisting in the Royal Marines. Towards the end of the following year he was wounded in Holland and invalided out of the army because of the seriousness of his injuries. After a slow recovery, he joined the Irish Guards in 1942, serving with the regiment in its North African campaign until he was again wounded, this time being taken prisoner. On another occasion, while undergoing training at a military camp in southern England, he was injured in both legs by bullets fired accidentally from an automatic weapon. But he survived both friend and enemy and, at the war's end, he was transferred to REME, whose troops were stationed, as part of the British Army of Occupation, at Glanmorgan Barracks, Duisburg, Germany.

In the same barracks was the man Emmett-Dunne was said to have killed, Reginald Walters. For officers of the court martial who had assembled to adjudicate on the Irishman's part in Walters's death, Glanmorgan Barracks was the place where the story began.

First the court heard from Griffith-Jones that an easy relationship existed between the civilian population and army personnel garrisoned at Duisburg. Many civilians worked at the base; there was plenty of social contact between the men and women of both groups, and the marriage of soldiers to local girls was quite a common event. One man who found romance in Duisburg was Sergeant

Walters. When the sergeant, an instructor at the technical training school, married his German girlfriend, an attractive cabaret entertainer, he moved from his bachelor army quarters to a flat about a mile from Glanmorgan Barracks. Walters and his wife, Maria, were on very friendly terms with Company-Sergeant-Major Emmett-Dunne, attached to No 4 Infantry Workshop, who was a regular visitor—too regular the prosecution claimed—at their flat. All three spent time together at outside functions and at parties in the sergeants' mess, where Emmett-Dunne devoted a lot of his time to his friend's wife. "Overdue attention" was how Griffith-Jones described it as he promised to produce witnesses who would testify to the existence of a clandestine affair between Emmett-Dunne and Maria Walters, which had begun in 1952.

Next to be related to the officers of the court were the events of 30 November 1953. Walters, said the prosecutor, left his home a little before 7.00p.m., telling his wife he would be back shortly. When he had not returned at 11.00p.m. Maria Walters phoned the barracks, asking if her husband was there or if anyone knew where he was. Nobody had seen the sergeant since sometime after 7.00p.m. when Emmett-Dunne said he had left him at the gate of the barracks. A neighbour of the Walterses called the orderly officer at 1.30a.m. making similar enquiries but there was still no news of the missing husband. A search of the base was made and at 3.00a.m. Emmett-Dunne, in company with the orderly officer, found Sergeant Walters hanging by a rope from the staircase of No 2 Barracks.

Continuing his address, Griffith-Jones described the outcome of the first autopsy and the suspicions of the army investigator which eventually led to the second. Then he referred to Ronald Emmett's statement to the police in England which, if believed by the court, would prove that Sergeant Walters had died not by his own hand but by that of the prisoner. In addition to calling the two pathologists, investigating detectives and Ronald Emmett, prosecuting counsel said he would be presenting other witnesses who would give supporting testimony to every aspect of the Crown's case. When it had heard and considered all the evidence, he said, he believed the court would come to the only reasonable conclusion possible, that the prisoner was guilty as charged.

The evidence the court listened to and considered lasted for seven days. As prosecuting counsel said they would, witnesses for the Crown told a story that seemed to point directly to the guilt of Emmett-Dunne, though there were some curious contradictions to be heard before the trial closed.

What the court learned was that Sergeant Walters and Emmett-Dunne were very close friends but their friendship had been showing signs of increasing strain in the weeks leading up to the sergeant's death. No one seemed to have any doubt as to the cause of an obvious tension that had developed in their relationship. All were agreed that Sergeant Walters objected to Emmett-Dunne's growing interest in Maria, particularly whenever the trio socialised together, as Maria would dance with the Irishman to the exclusion of her husband.

Mrs Ellen Kruger, the first witness called by Griffith-Jones, recalled Emmett-Dunne telling her after she had seen him dancing with Maria Walters that he was in love with a married woman. There would be no reason to question this story except for the fact that neither understood the other's language. Emmett-Dunne spoke no German, Ellen Kruger no English. It is one of the oddities of the case that went unquestioned and unexplained. Mrs Kruger's evidence, given through an interpreter, was not vital to either side; her testimony merely supported the prosecution's contention that CSM Emmett-Dunne and Maria Walters were having an affair. Just the same, it seems peculiar that Curtis-Bennett never asked this witness to explain how she and Emmett-Dunne had communicated. Later in the trial, in answer to a question put to him by his counsel, Emmett-

Dunne described Frau Kruger as little better than a whore. She had, he said, been chasing him for months and because he did not like her or her type, and had never given her a sideways glance, she had become vindictive, saying bad things about him. Whatever the truth of the matter, Curtis-Bennett, who needed every slight advantage he could get, failed to prise open this minor fault in the prosecutor's case. Proving Ellen Kruger to be untrustworthy would not in itself have altered the final outcome of the trial, but his failure to put pressure on the prosecution's first witness, exposing her evidence as unreliable, was a mistake, the first of a long series of errors that was to mar Derek Curtis-Bennett's conduct of the defence.

Emmett-Dunne frequently parked his car close by Walters's apartment where Maria would join him before going off with him. The pair would not return until late at night, when Emmett-Dunne would come with her into the flat. This evidence was given by the Crown's next witness, Mrs Bertha Ivens, who lived in the apartment immediately below the one occupied by Reginald and Maria Walters. These meetings took place while the sergeant was away on duty. This neighbour also saw the couple dancing on many occasions, she said, and added the gratuitous information that in her own mind she was positive they were in love.

Several acquaintances and friends had similar tales of secret meetings to relate to the court.

Evidence of Walters's concern with rumours that his wife and his friend were seeing a lot of each other in his absence was given by Staff Sergeant F Cracknell. This witness told of a conversation he had with Walters, who told him he thought something funny was going on between Emmett-Dunne and his wife. Although Cracknell scoffed at him for over-reacting to what was nothing more than gossip, from the amount of evidence heard in court it was clear that there was something more than talk involved and that Walters had good grounds for his fears.

When Sergeant Birmingham came to the witness-stand,

he was asked to identify a book handed to him by Griffith-Jones. The witness said it was a log-book used to keep a record of everyone entering or leaving Glanmorgan Barracks. On 30 November 1953, Sergeant Birmingham told the court, Emmett-Dunne was booked out at 7.05p.m. and logged back in again at a time he could not decipher, but which had been altered to read 7.20p.m.

It is hard to know what to make of this piece of evidence for it was not expanded upon by the prosecution, nor brought up in cross-examination by Curtis-Bennett. The implication seems to be that Emmett-Dunne, for his own advantage, changed the time of his return to the barracks. If this is so, it is not difficult to see why, and the impression left is one of deception on the part of the accused and should have been tackled by his counsel.

The prosecution's string of witnesses continued. Sergeant Stanley Kayne told of seeing Emmett-Dunne standing near the entrance to No 2 Block about 7.30p.m. on the night in question and William Barrett, who at that time worked as an orderly in the medical inspection room of No 2 Block, remembered seeing an object covered by a cape bundled inside the door of the block sometime after 7.00p.m. on that same night.

Then it was time for the prosecution's star witness. There was an air of expectancy in the court when Ronald Emmett was called to the witness-stand. Visibly nervous and ill at ease, Emmett was calmed by Brigadier Betts, who encouraged him to answer any question put to him by either counsel: "There is no danger of you being tried by court martial."

The witness first explained that he and the prisoner were half-brothers. At the time of Walters's death, he said, he was a private soldier serving with Emmett-Dunne at Duisburg and living in the same barracks. On the evening of 30 November 1953, Emmett received a message from Emmett-Dunne asking that the two should meet in the car park of the sergeants' mess about 8p.m. When he arrived there, his half-brother reminded him of their blood relationship and asked for his help, explaining that in the course of an argument he had killed a man. When Emmett enquired what had happened, Emmett-Dunne said that when he struck him, his friend fell dead at his feet. After the witness agreed to help him, Emmett-Dunne led the way to No 2 Block of the barracks, where inside the doorway lay the body of Sergeant Walters, covered by an army cape. Before they could move the corpse, sounds of approaching feet frightened Emmett, who rushed outside and concealed himself in some shrubbery. When he returned, he saw that Emmett-Dunne had fastened one end of a rope to the banister of the stairs. Together they lifted the body, Emmett-Dunne tying the other end of the rope around the neck of the dead sergeant. Emmett, who gave his evidence in a barely audible voice, was finally asked by Griffith-Jones if Emmett-Dunne had, at any time during the evening, complained of being attacked by Sergeant Walters.

"No sir, the only thing he said was: 'There's been an accident.'"

Ronald Emmett's motive for coming forward with his story was viewed by Curtis-Bennett with understandable scepticism. Emmett said his visit to the Hoylake police had no other cause than to see justice done. Defence counsel enquired if he had not gone to the police station "because you were scared stiff of being involved in some charge?" But the witness replied that, until he read of his half-brother's marriage, he had considered the whole matter above board. Only afterwards, he said, did he think that Sergeant Walters's death might not have been an accident. Published reports of the impending second autopsy, he claimed, had not influenced his decision one way or the other.

This assertion was a complete reversal of what he had told police in England, where he said a newspaper report of the probable exhumation of Reginald Walters's body had been the deciding factor in his change of mind.

Counsel for the defence expressed shocked disbelief but

his questioning of this witness was very weak and only reinforced the quiet assurance of Emmett, who had gained in confidence as his ordeal went on and seemed indifferent to whether or not his story sounded plausible.

It seems an obvious move for the defence to have asked Ronald Emmett at this stage if it was not the disinterment of Sergeant Walters's body that had motivated him to talk to the police, what *was* it that brought him into the open? After all, he had declared in his sworn confession—which, together with the medical evidence, became the core of the prosecution's case against the prisoner—that he saw nothing sinister in the wedding of Emmett-Dunne and Maria Walters. Also, it might have influenced the thinking of the officer of the tribunal to have known whether someone had guaranteed the witness immunity from prosecution if he testified against his half-brother, as Brigadier Betts's remarks to Emmett seemed to suggest. The brigadier's comment, of course, may have been nothing more than an attempt to calm a nervous man about to undergo a fairly intimidating experience. But no one was certain. Anyway, Curtis-Bennett ignored the opportunity and the questions were never asked.

Next to be described was the finding of Sergeant Walters's corpse. Griffith-Jones asked Quartermaster-Sergeant Charles Fry to recount for the court his part in its discovery. Fry said he was duty officer that night and he took a telephone call at 11p.m. from Mrs Walters enquiring about her husband. Nobody knew where he was. It was a second call at about 1.30a.m. from Mrs Ivens, who said Mrs Walters's husband was still missing, that led to a search of the camp. After a fruitless examination of the base, the duty officer was about to telephone Mrs Ivens when Emmett-Dunne suggested that, as Walters was friendly with an instructor billeted at the barracks' No 2 Block, enquiries at that building might be helpful. Entering together, they found Sergeant Walters's body suspended from the balustrade of the staircase. Lying on its side nearby was a bucket, seemingly kicked there in the last conscious action of the sergeant's life.

The body was later taken to the British military hospital, where an autopsy was performed by army pathologist Dr Alan Womack, who now told of his findings. Dr Womack discovered that the thyroid cartilage was fractured and had pierced the larynx, which was also fractured. Although they aroused no suspicion in his mind, the pathologist made two further discoveries that puzzled him. He considered the deep impression made by the rope to be slightly above the bruising on the neck, and the fact that the deceased had eaten a large meal shortly before death seemed unusual in a man contemplating the destruction of his own life. Still, despite these slight reservations, Dr Womack felt sure the sergeant's death was due to hanging and signed the death certificate to that effect. When an army court of enquiry agreed with his findings, he released the body for burial.

On the fourth day of the trial, Dr Francis Camps, the last witness called by the prosecution, enlivened the proceedings dramatically when he produced the late sergeant's larynx, visible in a clear container of preserving fluid. While giving evidence, the pathologist referred frequently to it and to diagrams of the throat and neck, enlarged several times for the purpose of demonstration.

Dr Camps informed the court that a fractured larynx was a very rare injury and could not have been caused by hanging. But experiments he had conducted showed the means that could produce it—a blow delivered across the front of the neck. Such a blow, however, if struck with a linear object like a broom-handle, would have left easily seen external marks. As no such marks were present on the sergeant's neck, except for some slight bruising, a smooth-surfaced pliable weapon must have been used. The doctor thought the edge of the hand, as used in unarmed combat, was the obvious answer.

When Curtis-Bennett rose to cross-examine he first asked Dr Camps if it would be possible to cause the death of a man by a light blow to the neck, "a blow that did not break the thyroid cartilage?"

"Oh yes, indeed."

Encouraged by this reply, counsel went on to suggest that the downward force of the hanging body might later have fractured the thyroid cartilage, in turn fracturing the larynx, but the pathologist would not agree to the suggestion:

"In my opinion, that could not happen."

To highlight the significance of this answer, the prosecutor re-examined Dr Camps, getting him to say that the damage to the thyroid cartilage and larynx could not have been caused by the rope. With this concluding assertion from the pathologist, Griffith-Jones's argument came to an end, making way for Emmett-Dunne's defence.

In his opening address to the court, Curtis-Bennett said the defendant's case would be that he had struck his friend with unintentional force, the action an impulse of self-preservation. In fright, he had staged the suicide, handling the situation with bad judgement and poor taste, but there was no suggestion that he had killed Sergeant Walters with malice.

The moment the court and spectators had been waiting for arrived when Emmett-Dunne took the oath and gave his version of events. Having first outlined his early life and army career, he was questioned by his counsel about his association with Maria Walters. He said that nothing improper had occurred, denying specifically that sexual intercourse had taken place between them. Maria and he were close friends, he admitted, but his friendship for her husband was just as strong, though he agreed that on the last night of his life Sergeant Walters doubted the truth of this fact. It was this mistrust that led to the tragedy of his friend's death, which Emmett-Dunne next described.

The two men had met near the entrance to No 2 Block, where Sergeant Walters appeared distressed and angry. Referring to his wife's relationship with Emmett-Dunne, Walters complained of being "fed up with playing second fiddle." Accepting an offer of a drive home, Walters got into the front passenger-seat of Emmett-Dunne's car and suddenly produced a revolver, which he brandished in front of the driver. Sergeant Walters claimed that Emmett-Dunne had shared a bed with Maria in Cologne the previous September, while he was engaged in military manoeuvres: "You think you can do anything but I'll put a stop to it." Emmett-Dunne told Walters that he was talking and behaving like a lunatic and pleaded with the sergeant to believe him when he said there was no truth in the allegations that he had made against him. Emmett-Dunne argued and implored Walters to listen to reason but the sergeant was becoming more agitated as the moments passed. Believing his life to be in imminent danger, Emmett-Dunne directed a sharp blow at the jaw of Walters, who collapsed in his seat, dropping the gun. By mere chance, he had misdirected the blow, which sadly resulted in the death of Walters. When he realised he had killed his friend, fearing that he might be accused of his murder, Emmett-Dunne panicked and dragged the body under the stairwell of No 2 Block, where later, with the aid of his half-brother, he faked the suicide.

This account may have been a true and accurate review of what had happened on the fatal night but, unfortunately for Emmett-Dunne, he proved to be an unimpressive witness on his own behalf. Even when guided by Curtis-Bennett, the accused man was often slow in his replies and on occasion seemed not to understand the questions. When recounting his transfer to Catterick, Yorkshire, soon after Sergeant Walters's death, and his accidental meeting there with Maria Walters, he was no more assured or convincing. His claim that he met Maria in a bar without any prior arrangement was highly improbable. Later, in his summing-up, the judge-advocate, Charles Cahn, said: "By any account this was a remarkable story." And so it was. No one could believe that Emmett-Dunne called by pure chance to the Ingrams Arms Hotel, Leeds, to find it managed by Sergeant Walters's sister, who at that moment was being visited by the sergeant's widow from Germany.

As it was already established that a probable intimate relationship existed between the pair, it was a needless fabrication. And the danger of the court's not believing Emmett-Dunne should have been anticipated by Curtis-Bennett, as it put in question everything else said by his client.

Following further meetings at which Emmett-Dunne spoke of compensating for the loss of Maria's husband, the couple were married at a Leeds registry office on 3 June 1954. Demobilised by the army, Emmett-Dunne with his wife moved to Somerset to start a new life.

In answering the remaining few questions of his counsel, Emmett-Dunne surely shredded what was left of his credibility. Curtis-Bennett brought him back to the night of the tragedy and asked him to explain his feelings when he realised his friend was dead. Emmett-Dunne said he was deeply shocked, frightened and then dejected at what he knew would be his certain discharge from the army, the army which had been his whole life. Earlier, for Griffith-Jones, a Mrs Bannerman gave evidence of Emmett-Dunne's frequent use of her telephone to call Mrs Walters while her husband was away. Now Curtis-Bennett, who persisted at every hand's turn to dismiss any suggestion of an illicit liaison between his client and Maria Walters, asked Emmett-Dunne to explain these calls. He explained that because of trouble he was having over suspicions of his involvement in the disappearance of some mess funds, he was going to desert. Mrs Walters, he said, was making travel and currency arrangements for his departure—hence the many calls.

Immediately after expressing his sadness at the prospect of being forced to leave the army, Emmett-Dunne had given a reply to his counsel's question that left the courtroom in silent disbelief.

And he performed even less well under the vigorous cross-examination of Griffith-Jones, though he told substantially the same story to the prosecutor. His answers were again given in an uncertain and hesitant manner, prompting prosecution counsel to remark that he must have something to hide. Emmett-Dunne denied this was so and, becoming increasingly irritated by the persistent prodding of Griffith-Jones, entered into a furious wrangle with the prosecutor over what he termed the senseless questions being put to him. If he was asked sensible questions, he said, he would be pleased to give sensible answers. It was unwise of Emmett-Dunne to have allowed himself to become enmeshed in an exchange that could only end one way. Overall, in his performance before his own counsel and in cross-examination by Griffith-Jones, he was made to look foolish, unreliable and unconvincing.

His wife, on the other hand, made a very good impression when she took the witness-stand, even though she gave the impression of having a rather prudish attitude on sexual matters. She confirmed all that Emmett-Dunne had said about their relationship being one of friendship. But the unwholesome notion of the prosecution that she and Emmett-Dunne had engaged in sexual intercourse scandalised Maria out of her senses, causing an interruption to the proceedings while she was given some water. Regaining her composure, she asserted that during the lifetime of her former husband nothing illicit had ever occurred between herself and the prisoner. In spite of all the reports, rumours and gossip of an adulterous affair, journalists covering the court martial believed that Maria's evidence, given to both counsel, was generally sound.

Closing speeches for defence and prosecution followed along expected lines. For the defence, Curtis-Bennett said there was a lack of real evidence of sexual liaison between his client and the victim's wife. All that the prosecution had managed to do was to unearth a lot of gossip. He then went on to belittle the accuracy and relevance of the pathologist's testimony, saying that the blow struck by Emmett-Dunne, though fatal, was purely accidental; all the Crown's evidence, including its questionable medical theories, had failed to prove otherwise. Finally, counsel asked the officers of the court if they could say precisely how Sergeant Walters had met his death. If they were unable to do so, he suggested, "the only thing you can do to satisfy your honour is to acquit Emmett-Dunne."

The prosecutor, Griffith-Jones, who aired different views, was quite certain in his mind how Sergeant Walters had died. He had been brutally murdered by Emmett-Dunne and the balance of the sworn testimony of witnesses pointed unmistakably to that fact. First of all, there was the undoubted evidence of a love affair. Yet the defendant denied its existence. What belief could be placed in anything else he might say? Were the actions of Emmett-Dunne the actions of an innocent man? The prosecutor did not think so. Why had the prisoner not gone to find a doctor or medical orderly? Emmett-Dunne's answer that he had panicked was not a believable explanation from a combat-hardened soldier who had seen death in many forms. Counsel for the prosecution ended by saying he had every confidence the court would bring in the correct verdict, based on the overwhelming probabilities of the Crown's presentation.

Summarising the case, Mr Charles Cahn, the judge-advocate, went over the evidence point by point but, apart from his remarks concerning Emmett-Dunne's unlikely meeting with Maria in Leeds, he highlighted just one other piece of testimony which, he thought, the court should consider most carefully. On the second day of the trial, Sergeant Thomas Brown had told Mr Griffith-Jones that, a month or so before the death of Sergeant Walters, Emmett-Dunne had said to him: "There is a certain person in our mess who will commit suicide if his wife doesn't behave herself." The court, thought Mr Cahn, might consider this remark proof of premeditation on the part of the prisoner.

The summing-up on 7 July did nothing to cheer Emmett-Dunne, who was led from the courtroom while his fate was being decided. Just over an hour later, he was back in court to hear the verdict of Guilty read to him. He showed no emotion at the announcement that he was to die by hanging.

But he was not executed. As capital punishment was no longer in force in Germany, he had his sentence, which he served in England, changed to one of life imprisonment.

His marriage did not survive his detention. In 1964 he was granted a divorce on the grounds of adultery by Maria, a charge she did not contest. Frederick Emmett-Dunne was released from prison in July 1966.

9

THE ADAMS CASE

Dr John Bodkin Adams   London, 1957

On Wednesday, 22 August 1956, most newspapers in Britain found space to report the result of an inquest held the previous day at Eastbourne in Sussex. The enquiry, chaired by the East Sussex coroner, Dr AC Sommerville, was to establish the cause of death of Mrs Gertrude Joyce Hullett, a fifty-year-old local woman who had died at her home on 23 July. After hearing medical evidence that Mrs Hullett had died of an overdose of barbiturate sleeping pills, and had previously spoken of taking her own life, the jury brought in a verdict of suicide.

The jury had also heard how the family physician, Dr John Adams, had received £1000 from Mrs Hullett shortly before her death, and had been left a Rolls-Royce car in Mrs Hullett's will. The coroner had gone on severely to criticise Dr Adams for his treatment of the patient. He was especially critical of the doctor's failure to engage professional daytime help, his unwillingness to call in psychiatric assistance when Mrs Hullett's rapidly deteriorating mental condition obviously demanded it and his poor judgement in not moving the patient to hospital. Dr Adams's response was that he had done all that he thought best, and to assembled journalists and news photographers he said as he left the court: "The result of the inquest has cleared up all the ugly rumours and innuendos which have been going about."

He was mistaken. The same day that the inquest proceedings were reported, the *Daily Mail* was informing its readers of a massive investigation being undertaken by Scotland Yard's murder squad into the mass murder of wealthy women during the past twenty years: "the most sensational investigation of the country's criminal history." The police were particularly interested in the wills of persons who had left valuable estates and of any suspicious circumstances surrounding their deaths. Also to be investigated were the beneficiaries of each individual will. Further sensational revelations were confidently expected, concluded the article. Strangely, it was the French magazine, *Paris Match*, which first broke the story of suspicious deaths in Eastbourne, but the British press, a little hesitant at first, correctly sensed the direction of popular feeling and jumped on the bandwagon. The *Daily Mail*'s report was only one of many, all of which revived earlier rumours and gossip which fanned the fires of sinister speculation. The rumours had grown from mild surprise expressed at the number of deaths among the doctor's elderly women patients to what amounted almost to an accusation of mass poisoning. Eventually, public pressure forced the Eastbourne police to open enquiries into the allegations and their chief constable, James Walker, asked Scotland Yard to assist them.

Detective Superintendent Herbert Hannan of the Scotland Yard Murder Squad took charge of the investigation and was assisted by Detective Sergeant Charlie Hewitt from the same unit. Their enquiries continued into December.

When Dr Adams heard the police were about to exhume two former patients of his, he contacted the Medical Defence Union who immediately engaged the pathologist, Professor Keith Simpson, to be present as an observer when Professor Francis Camps examined the remains for the Crown. Nothing incriminating was discovered. In the first instance, the condition of the body precluded any possibility of establishing the cause of death, while study of the second corpse confirmed that death was due to cerebral thrombosis, as originally certified by Dr Adams.

Scotland Yard was not discouraged at what it saw as a temporary set-back. After several meetings with the Attorney-General and the Director of Public Prosecutions in London, Hannan was finally instructed to arrest the doctor for the murder of yet another of his late patients, Mrs Edith Morrell. The superintendent travelled back to Eastbourne on 19 December 1956, where he arrested and charged the doctor with Mrs Morrell's death which took place on 13 November 1950. Not all those following the investigation by the police were surprised at the news, which became the subject of banner headlines in the national press the following morning. The subsequent trial made Dr Adams's name known throughout the world.

The man who was now the focus of the world's press was born John Bodkin Adams in 1899 in Co Antrim, Ireland. He attended school at Coleraine and later enrolled as a medical student at Queen's University, Belfast, where he qualified in 1921. His first professional experience was gained at a hospital in Bristol, where he stayed only a short time before moving to Eastbourne to work as a junior partner with two established physicians, Dr Gurney and Dr Emerson. He quickly made a name for himself as an efficient and caring doctor untroubled by long hours or night calls. In time, he built for himself a substantial private practice, mostly of elderly wealthy patients who lived out their retirement in comfort in the many nursing homes in the popular coastal resort. In his thirty-five years in the town, Dr Adams was generally well liked by a wide circle of friends and acquaintances, among them the chairman of the Eastbourne magistrates, Dr Roland Gwynne, and Eastbourne's chief constable, James Walker, who had the disagreeable duty of helping to bring the charge of murder against him. Those critical of Adams claimed he was mean in matters of money and often dressed in an ostentatious way. That he drove high-powered, showy motorcars upset some. Others thought

Dr Adams a religious crank. At the time of his trial he was a man of established social status and an unlikely candidate to fill the role of poisoner in a case that had already intrigued and fascinated the public imagination.

On 18 March 1957 the trial of Dr John Bodkin Adams for the murder of Mrs Edith Morrell began in the Central Criminal Court before Sir Patrick Devlin. The trial had some unusual features. It was to become the longest murder trial in English legal history; its principal actor, Dr Adams, having pleaded "not guilty," never spoke another word for the seventeen days' duration of the hearing; the crime with which he was charged had taken place six years previously; and the Crown did not have the body of the victim, for, in accordance with her own wishes, Mrs Morrell had been cremated. Also strange was the absence of the customary pre-trial betting among members of the press. They, it seemed, were in agreement with their millions of readers—the doctor would be convicted as charged.

The Attorney-General, Sir Reginald Manningham-Buller QC—whom critics claimed was more interested in politics than in law—led for the Crown. Dr Adams was defended by Mr Geoffrey Lawrence QC, known to be an able lawyer but one who had not previously acted as a defence counsel in a murder trial. Some misgivings were expressed at the time about the choice of counsel to fight the doctor's case, but most correspondents thought he would start slowly and gradually develop confidence as the trial progressed, giving a good account of himself in the end. He certainly did that.

The case for the prosecution rested almost exclusively on the testimony of their specialist medical expert and on the evidence of four nurses who had attended Mrs Morrell during the time of her final illness. Crown counsel seemed to have taken it for granted that the nurses' stories as told in the magistrates' court would simply be repeated without challenge at the Old Bailey and that the claims of expert witness, Dr Arthur Doubtwaite, at the same hearing could now be safely reiterated without serious dispute. But, as it transpired, the business of the medical evidence was not as cut and dried as expected.

What the nurses told the magistrates was that even when their patient was in a deep coma, morphia and heroin had been administered on Dr Adams's instructions and that on several occasions the doctor himself had given large injections to Mrs Morrell, though they did not know what they were. Dr Doubtwaite had no doubts when giving his testimony. He said that, making allowance for the seriously weakened condition of the patient, the amount of drugs given could have been administered only with the intention of killing her. Such damning evidence from so acknowledged a specialist had placed Dr Adams in the dock.

Now, on the first morning of the trial, the Attorney-General was indicating what the prosecution would hope to prove. The story he told was substantially the same as that heard at the preliminary hearing before the magistrates. In opening the Crown's case against Adams, the prosecutor informed the jury that, in addition to being a Bachelor of Surgery, the accused was also a qualified and practising anaesthetist. It was reasonable, therefore, to suppose that he could not be ignorant of the effects of drugs on the human system. Referring to Mrs Morrell, the Attorney-General said she was an eighty-one-year-old wealthy woman whose estate at the time of her death was valued at £157 000. A stroke suffered in 1948 left her paralysed down her left side and in constant need of medical attention, which was supplied in the persons of Dr Adams and four nurses. The nurses would come forward to tell them that at no time did they see their patient in pain. Yet vast quantities of drugs were given to Mrs Morrell in the form of morphia and heroin, both of which substances were well known to be addictive. Why had those drugs been administered? The Attorney-General suggested the jury might feel that the motive concerned changes made in Mrs Morrell's will. The accused, he said, was not included as a beneficiary in the original will of the deceased but, on the doctor's suggestion to him, Mr Sagno, her solicitor, prepared a codicil which Mrs Morrell had requested and signed, leaving Dr Adams some silver in a carved oak chest and, should her son die before her, a Rolls-Royce car and an antique cupboard. Was it not sinister that while he was prescribing unnecessary quantities of drugs for her, he was at the same time concerning himself with the last testament of his patient? And, Manningham-Buller pointed out, the jury should take special note that in the last fortnight of her life, prescriptions for morphia increased three times and heroin sevenfold compared with any previous two weeks of her illness.

All this was soundly impressive stuff that any jury would understand but Sir Reginald was on far shakier ground with his submission that the doctor had killed his patient to stop her from changing her will again. The doctor, he said, decided Mrs Morrell must die so that "...she should have no further opportunity for altering her will." Journalists shook their heads in doubt and the jury of ten men and two women probably thought that there must be more to it than that, as they listened to the Attorney-General's address. Finally, he called attention to the night of Mrs Morrell's death, when the nurse gave her two injections—very large ones—both prepared by Dr Adams. There was absolute silence in the court as Crown counsel, showing just how large these injections were, held in the air a 5cc syringe with a dramatic flourish, as the jury looked speculatively at Adams in the dock. Why were these two injections given to an already unconscious patient? Answering his own question, the Attorney-General said there could only be one reason, to bring about the death of Mrs Morrell, and he was confident that the jury would come to the same conclusion.

The formal evidence from four pharmacists of compounding medicines and filling prescriptions for Dr Adams was not challenged by the defence, and the first important witness of the trial was Nurse Helen Stronach, who was questioned by junior counsel for the Crown, Mr

Melford Stephenson. After she had indicated her hours of duty, Stephenson asked her to describe for the jury the medical procedure followed when she was caring for Mrs Morrell. Complying with Dr Adams's instructions, she said, she gave the patient a quarter-grain of morphia each evening at 9.00p.m.; then, at about 11.00p.m., while Mrs Morrell was still in a dopey condition, the doctor would call and give her another injection. She could not say what was in the doctor's injections.

When he rose to cross-examine her Mr Lawrence asked the nurse if a written report was made at the time of Mrs Morrell's illness six years earlier.

"We noted down every injection we gave. We reported everything."

Then, the seemingly irrelevant question:

"So that, if only we had those reports now, we could see the truth of exactly what happened night by night and day by day when you were there?"

"Yes, but you have our word for it."

Geoffrey Lawrence then mesmerised his audience with what the usually staid *Times* headlined as a "Surprise Development in Adams Trial." From the defence table he produced the books and asked the bewildered Miss Stronach to identify them. The Attorney-General jumped to his feet but seemed too astonished to say anything and sat down again. Although neither he nor anybody else had yet a precise idea what significance these medical records would have on the trial, they were soon to learn.

While the nurse's recollection had Mrs Morrell as rambling and semi-conscious, the medical report showed the patient to have consumed "a lunch of a small quantity of partridge, a small quantity of celery, a small quantity of pudding and a small quantity of brandy and soda." At a time when Nurse Stronach remembered Mrs Morrell as being in a coma, her own written account had the patient "continued talking and asking for drinks until past midnight." When Mr Lawrence had spent some time reading aloud the entries of Nurse Stronach, he said that he had gone over every word of the whole record for the relevant time and nowhere was there a single instance of her having given a quarter-grain of morphia; on the couple of occasions when the doctor did give injections they were known to be paraldehyde. Defence counsel used his severest voice when he suggested to the witness that her memory was playing tricks on her. There were few reporters present to hear her reply, "I have nothing to say." Most had already left the court to telephone the story of Lawrence's conjuring trick with medical reports to their editors. Although the Attorney-General tried to rehabilitate the witness by recalling Nurse Stronach to the witness-box, there was no recovering the lost advantage.

Dr Adams's counsel was more than just an exponent of courtroom wizardry, as suggested by some of the popular newspapers. He left nothing to chance. With meticulous care, he went through the remaining medical records with each nurse, proving conclusively that their recollections were unreliable. Just as easily as he had shattered the credibility of Nurse Stronach's evidence, Mr Lawrence destroyed the value of Sister Mason-Ellis's testimony when he came to cross-examine her, though even before that Sir Reginald was having difficulties with his own witness. Following unhelpful replies to several of his questions, he finally referred to Mrs Morrell and, in desperation, asked: "Could you tell us something of her general condition?"

Sister Mason-Ellis could not. Clearly upset, the nurse answered that it was too long ago.

"Honestly, it was six years."

But when Lawrence took over the witness, he soon elicited the answers he sought. Having reminded her of her earlier claim that Mrs Morrell had been in a coma, counsel read an entry of the sister's for the day before the patient's death: "Awake but quiet, half a glass of milk and brandy."

"So, when you wrote 'awake' she must have been awake?"

"She must have been!"

"Therefore, she could not possibly be in a coma."

A dejected Mason-Ellis was replaced in the witness-box by Dr Walker, medical referee at Brighton crematorium, who gave evidence of the cremation form of Mrs Morrell. He was followed by the third of the nurses, Nurse Randall, who fared no better than her colleagues under Geoffrey Lawrence's relentless cross-examination. Earlier, the Attorney-General made Mrs Randall review the events of the patient's last hours. The nurse said that, except for brief spells, the patient was in a coma. Dr Adams called at about 10.00p.m. that evening, filled a syringe with an unknown preparation and instructed her to inject the contents into the still-unconscious patient. She did as she was told. The doctor then refilled the syringe and told her to give this injection later to Mrs Morrell if she had not become quiet. She gave this second injection, much against her will, she stressed, having failed to contact the doctor by telephone.

Counsel for the accused told the witness he wanted first to deal with a time in September when Dr Adams went away on his annual holiday and the care of the patient was left to his partner, Dr Harris. Mr Lawrence read aloud from Nurse Randall's own written record the quantities of drugs given to Mrs Morrell during this period, which on occasions exceeded those recommended by Dr Adams. Emphasising this fact, Lawrence asked the nurse was it not now obvious from her own notes that "Dr Harris continued to use the same drugs as Dr Adams had been using?"

"Yes."

Defence counsel next wanted to know why there was no reference in her medical record to the telephone call she said she had made to Adams. Why had she described Mrs Morrell as being in a coma when her report noted the patient to be "restless, talkative and very shaky. Paraldehyde 5cc given by doctor"? And how was it, asked counsel, that there was no written report of her second injection, if she actually gave it? To this last question, she insisted, "I did give it."

"You cannot have it both ways. If it was a matter of any

importance, it would have gone into the book?"

"Yes."

After some further exchanges, defence counsel remarked:

"Your memory is not trustworthy, is it?"

"It appears not to be."

The last of the nursing witnesses, Sister Bartlett, followed the pattern of her colleagues in claiming that Mrs Morrell had been semi-conscious or in a coma in the days immediately before her death. Mr Lawrence read from this witness's medical notes: "Aware, talkative, restless, milk and brandy taken." He then compelled Sister Bartlett to agree that her written notes, made as events unfolded, were correct and her earlier evidence was not. He finally enquired if every effort had been made under the doctor's instructions to keep the patient as mobile as possible. Sister Bartlett said yes, and her reply brought to an end the first week of the trial.

Five days earlier, the mass of the Crown's evidence, as outlined by Sir Reginald, looked beyond argument but its hidden weaknesses were exposed with the production of the nurses' medical records. What at first seemed clear and sure was shown by Geoffrey Lawrence to be dangerously inaccurate. It was now quite obvious that if the Attorney-General was going to build a convincing case against Adams, it would not be on the basis of the nurses' evidence. Despite the embarrassment of this evidence to the Crown, its star witness was yet to appear and what he might say was looked forward to with great interest, but first Lawrence wanted some information from the Crown's next witness, Mr Sagno, Mrs Morrell's solicitor.

The prosecution alleged that Dr Adams had murdered his patient for her property which he would receive under her will.

"Had Mrs Morrell altered the provision of her previous will to include the doctor?" enquired Adams's counsel.

"She did not."

The impact of this answer was immediate and stunned

the court. Making sure the significance of the reply was not lost on the jury, Lawrence hammered home the point.

"So that when she died in November the doctor was not in any way a beneficiary under her will?"

"That is correct."

"For anything at all?"

"For nothing at all."

At a time when many observers thought it would have ended, the trial had still eleven days to run, but already the prosecution's case was falling about the Attorney-General's ears. Despite high expectations, he gained no advantage from the testimony of his next two witnesses, Eastbourne's Detective Inspector Pugh and Scotland Yard's Detective Superintendent Hannan. It was no secret that Sir Reginald intended completely to destroy Adams's defence when the time came to cross-examine the doctor but for now, if he was to salvage anything from the ruins of the nurses' medical evidence, his principal witness, Dr Doubtwaite, would have to be his saviour.

Dr Arthur Doubtwaite was Senior Physician and a highly regarded teacher of therapeutics at London's Guy's Hospital.

Mrs Morrell had suffered a stroke earlier in her life and Sir Reginald came quickly to this point in his questioning of the medical expert. He asked Dr Doubtwaite whether there was justification for injecting morphia and heroin into an invalid after such an occurrence.

"No justification whatsoever."

"Is it right or wrong to do so?"

"Wrong. In all circumstances, wrong."

Here were unhesitant answers given with such a ring of absolute authority that everyone in the court was suddenly alert. And the witness gave many more answers, all equally emphatic, during his direct examination, his cross-examination and his questioning by Mr Justice Devlin. In all, the Crown's narcotics specialist spent four days in the witness-box, displaying extraordinary physical and mental stamina and a hugely inflated ego.

Replying to further queries by prosecution counsel, Dr Doubtwaite asserted that morphia given after a stroke would not only be unhelpful but would greatly interfere with the rehabilitation of the patient. He stressed, in fact, that sedation of someone who had suffered a stroke was not necessary nor in general was it desirable, other than as a treatment for acute mania, when one morphia injection might be given. When asked about the use of heroin in similar circumstances, Dr Doubtwaite's opinion was that, except in cases of incurable disease, heroin should not be given to persons over the age of seventy. Even more decisive was his response when asked what legitimate medical reason there was for giving regular doses of morphia and heroin to so aged a patient as Mrs Morrell:

"There isn't one."

Dr Doubtwaite was a devastating witness for the Crown. At the conclusion of his examination, it seemed that rarely was a prosecution blessed with such positive expert testimony.

A little before 11.00a.m. on the ninth day of the trial, Lawrence rose to cross-examine the Crown's specialist. When Lawrence asked him if he knew where Mrs Morrell had had a stroke in 1948, Dr Doubtwaite said he understood it had happened in Cheshire while she was holidaying with her son. Had Dr Doubtwaite accurate information about Mrs Morrell's treatment while in hospital in Cheshire, enquired counsel, or were "attempts made to furnish you with it before you reached your final conclusion?" Slightly nettled by Lawrence's gentle prodding, the expert answered:

"I did not regard it as my duty to find out facts of that sort."

But Geoffrey Lawrence did. He held up a document which he said he wanted the witness to examine. He had done it again! Just as with the nurses' medical reports which he produced with sensational effect early in the trial, the Cheshire hospital records now materialised as if by magic. Reading from the document, Mr Lawrence advised Dr

Doubtwaite that, while she was hospitalised in Cheshire, two doctors, Dr Pemberton and Dr Turner, had treated Mrs Morrell with morphia. This was not a solitary injection administered to control a period of acute mania but a quarter-grain dose given regularly night after night for the ten days' duration of Mrs Morrell's stay. The courtroom came alive with this new evidence, which must have been a perplexing distraction for the jury who for two days had heard Dr Doubtwaite state categorically and reiterate *ad nauseam* that morphia must under no circumstances be used in the treatment of a patient after a stroke, except at a time of acute mania. But now there was sworn and documented testimony that altogether four doctors had given Mrs Morrell morphia as part of her after-stroke treatment, Dr Pemberton and Dr Turner in Cheshire—who first introduced the drug—and Dr Adams and Dr Harris in Eastbourne, who continued with its use. And, as defence counsel pointed out to the Crown's specialist, three of the doctors were not being charged with murder. In the light of this new information Lawrence enquired of Doubtwaite: "Does the field of condemnation that you are spreading from the witness-box include Dr Turner of Cheshire?"

"If that was the treatment for the stroke, yes."

Dr Doubtwaite held tenaciously to his opinion. No matter how often Lawrence re-phrased and repeated the question, the Crown's medical expert refused to be forced into an admission that the four doctors might possibly have been correct in their treatment and that he might possibly be wrong in his assessment of their behaviour. Even the judge, who frequently took over the questioning of the witness and who was clearly anxious to clarify Dr Doubtwaite's thinking, made as little progress as defence counsel. At one point, when Lawrence was referring to the retention of morphia in the patient's body, which Dr Doubtwaite believed was part of Adams's murderous plan to bring about the death of Mrs Morrell, Mr Justice Devlin enquired: "If another doctor were to say he disagreed entirely with your view on accumulation, would that be a skilled genuine view to the contrary?"

"I can only say I would be astonished if he does."

If he felt any uneasiness at the judge's persistent interventions to question him, Dr Doubtwaite showed no sign. Nor did he seem aware that the unbending certainty of his pronouncements and his mulish refusal to consider any view but his own was antagonising the jury and bringing despair to the Crown's barristers. Long before the judge summarised Dr Doubtwaite's four days of evidence the distinguished physician's credibility was in smithereens.

"You say the treatment could not have been due to error, ignorance or incompetence and must have been due to an intent to kill?"

"That is my view."

"It must follow that anybody who expresses a view contrary to yours is expressing a view that he cannot honestly hold?"

"Yes."

This was not quite the view of the next two medical witnesses. The prosecution's second medical specialist, Dr Michael Ashby, a consultant neurologist to several London hospitals, thought the quantities of drugs given to Mrs Morrell by Dr Adams were excessive. But he would not say they were given with the intention of terminating life—which was precisely what Adams was charged with. To the suggestion of Mr Lawrence that Mrs Morrell might have died of natural causes, Dr Ashby replied that such a possibility could not be ruled out. Dr Ashby was the prosecution's last witness.

The court was immediately brought to attention by Lawrence on the thirteenth morning of the proceedings when he approached the bench and asked the judge not to let the trial go any further. Mr Justice Devlin agreed to hear counsel's argument and ordered that the jury be taken from the courtroom. In a lengthy submission Lawrence contended that the Crown's case was based wholly on expert medical evidence, all of which had been totally discredited in cross-examination and further demolished by certified clinical records. Also, their case was undermined to a large degree by the testimony of Dr Ashby, one of the prosecution's own experts. After some consideration, the judge said he believed that there was enough evidence to put before the jury. The motion was denied.

If Lawrence had surprised his listeners in the morning, the shock was mild compared with what he had waiting for them in the afternoon. The court was still settling in following the luncheon recess when he said his first witness would be Dr John Harman, consulting physician at St Thomas's Hospital in London, adding almost casually that he had decided "in the circumstances not to call the doctor [Adams]." The short announcement generated vast reaction, especially among the prosecution team, whose members were visibly shocked, and some newspapermen, who once again ran hotfoot in search of telephones.

Mr Lawrence now examined the one and only witness for the defence. Dr Harman declared that he saw nothing sinister in the quantities of drugs prescribed for Mrs Morrell by Dr Adams, as he himself had often administered similar amounts of morphia to elderly patients of his own. From the evidence he had heard he was convinced that there was no criminal design in Dr Adams's treatment of his patient. Dr Harman did not alter his opinions under cross-examination.

So there it was, the end of the seemingly endless medical evidence. Dr Doubtwaite was absolutely certain that Dr Adams had meant to kill Mrs Morrell; on the other hand, Dr Michael Ashby was not sure what Adams's intentions had been, while Dr Harman was quite positive that Dr Adams's treatment of his patient had been perfectly normal medical practice. For the jury it was all very confusing but they were not overwhelmed.

Juries are notoriously sceptical of experts and expert evidence, often with clear justification. The Adams murder trial produced some examples of the reasons for such suspicions. Dr Doubtwaite's egocentricity while giving evidence was exceptional but by no means unique for a testifying specialist, nor was he the only specialist to make a fool of himself during the trial: Lawrence's sole witness, Dr Harman, had also, for a while at least, managed to make himself appear just as idiotic. While answering Lawrence on a question of the effects of morphia convulsions, Dr Harman suddenly began to shake all over. With his body bent forward from the waist, his head began jerking violently from side to side as his eyes stared wildly from his purple face and his palms shot forward repeatedly as if to disperse demons. Accompanying these graphic gyrations with animal-like sounds, Dr Harman was assured of the court's attention, although it was noticed that the judge never moved a muscle during the drama of the whole display.

Mr Justice Devlin, of course, had met a good many experts. It was an arresting performance which received wide coverage in the evening editions. Then, the following morning, while under cross-examination, Dr Harman was compelled to admit to the Attorney-General that he had never in his life seen a single case of morphia convulsions. What the jury thought of Dr Harman's pantomime is unknown but there are no doubts about how they viewed Dr Doubtwaite's performance.

Opposing sides made closing speeches along expected lines before Mr Justice Devlin reviewed the case for the jury, whose deliberations lasted three-quarters of an hour. When they returned to find the prisoner "not guilty," journalists with deadlines to meet shouldered spectators and trampled each other in a wild rush to relay the news of Dr Adams's acquittal. The jury, after seventeen days' service, was thanked for performing its civic duty and released, and Dr John Adams, having spent 111 days in detention, was given his freedom.

Despite the dramatic stampeding of correspondents, the verdict could have surprised very few. Long before the trial dragged to its end, the Crown's case was in shreds and, for all his fiery oratory on side issues, the Attorney-General could not obscure the glaring deficiencies of his case. According to Sir Reginald in his opening speech, Dr Adams had introduced Mrs Morrell to morphia so as to exercise his power over her. The Attorney-General was wise to avoid this issue in his closing address, for the evidence proved conclusively that Mrs Morrell was prescribed this drug originally by two doctors attending her in Cheshire and Dr Adams had merely continued the same treatment. Greed was claimed by the Crown to be the motive for Adams's murderous actions. By using his position he influenced his patient to change her will in his favour. But her own solicitor swore under oath that the doctor had received nothing under his client's will, although Dr Adams was given some silver in a chest and a motorcar by Mrs Morrell's son, who believed his mother wished him to do so as a gesture of gratitude. The Attorney-General's most damning allegation, that the doctor had personally injected his patient with poisonous substances, was clearly contradicted by the evidence of his own witnesses' written records. The jury learned that nothing more lethal had been administered by Dr Adams than paraldehyde, a recognised product regularly used to induce sleep.

The Attorney-General's lack of preparation for the trial is difficult to understand. The popular press presented Geoffrey Lawrence as a miracle-worker but his willingness to pursue every possibility that might benefit his client was a better reason for his acclaimed success. Another and more obvious cause was that the medical witnesses had to withstand his devastating cross-examination and none of them managed to survive the ordeal. This was particularly true of Dr Doubtwaite, the Crown's leading expert, whom Lawrence succeeded in turning into a powerful witness for the defence. A rare achievement. Altogether Lawrence's handling of the case was quite brilliant; but really, the extraordinary ineptitude of the Crown's research and planning for the trial contributed enormously to the eventual outcome.

It would not have been a difficult task to check the provision of Mrs Morrell's will yet the prosecution never did so. The Crown also unaccountably neglected to acquaint itself with Mrs Morrell's earlier medical history, information that was of vital importance at the trial. But by far the greatest tactical error was the Attorney-General's absolute belief in his ability in cross-examination to tear asunder Dr Adams's claim of innocence. When Lawrence advised his client against giving evidence on his own behalf, then Sir Reginald was deprived of his chance to question Adams under oath. He should have foreseen the possibility of such an eventuality. The débâcle that was the balance of the Crown's case could not possibly sustain a conviction and Mr Justice Devlin, openly incredulous of some of the Attorney-General's presentation, said as much when he told the jury that, "the case for the defence seems to me a manifestly strong one."

Dr Adams was later charged under the Dangerous Drugs Act for over-prescribing drugs. As a result of his conviction he was struck from the Medical Register but later had his name restored. He went home to Eastbourne and continued to care for a small number of elderly ladies who remained loyal to him. But the shadow of guilt was never fully removed from his name in the minds of many of his former patients. Of the great majority of those familiar with the investigation—local police officers, Scotland Yard Murder Squad detectives and veteran crime-reporters—almost all believed Dr Adams was a mass murderer. Only on the number of his victims did they differ; some thought he had poisoned eight of his patients, while others were convinced the figure was nearer twenty. Probably the truth will never be known. All that can confidently be said is that the Attorney-General, Sir Reginald Manningham-Buller, made an unbelievably inept job of proving Dr Adams guilty of murdering one of his elderly patients, Mrs Edith Morrell.

Dr Adams lived out his life quietly, finding amusement in clay-pigeon shooting, at which he became an expert. He died in Eastbourne in 1983.

10

THE BIRMINGHAM HOSTEL MURDER

Patrick Byrne   Birmingham, 1960

The most brutal single murder ever investigated by the Birmingham city police was that of Stephanie Baird, who was strangled on 23 December 1959. The subsequent search for her killer became one of the greatest man-hunts mounted in England.

The case began for the police at 7.30p.m. that December evening with a 999 call to Birmingham police headquarters. The caller reported an attack by a male intruder on a young woman at a hostel in the Edgbaston area of the city.

Responding to the alert, a patrol car with Constables Cowley and Whiting went to the YWCA hostel in Wheeleys Road, where they found Margaret Brown, one of the residents, in a distressed condition. She had received a scalp wound but her injuries were not serious. She was able to tell the patrolmen that she had gone to a room at the back of the house to do some ironing, when she had heard a noise, went to investigate and was attacked when she opened a door leading into a washroom. Her instinctive move to one side as her assailant rushed forward probably saved her life. Her terrified screams frightened off her attacker, who left behind the large stone he had used as a weapon.

The officers, after relaying a description of the prowler back to headquarters, searched the grounds of the house but discovered no intruder. They also examined the annexe in the grounds, a prefabricated structure known as the Queen's Wing, where all but one of the twelve rooms in the building were found to be empty. Room No 4, as one of the residents had reported to the police, was locked from the inside. She said she had received no answer to her knocking. Neither did Constable Moore, who had arrived at the hostel to assist Cowley and Whiting. To prevent the possible escape of a prowler, Constable Cowley went to the back of the annexe. As he was entering the locked room through the window, Moore broke down the door with his shoulder. When the lights were switched on, the officers were frozen into shock with the enormity of the sight that confronted them. For a few moments they were unable to trust the evidence of their own eyes.

The naked body lying on the floor was that of a young woman whose head and right breast had been cut off and placed on the bed. The headless body had been subjected to further mutilations with lines scored the length of the trunk. Also visible were several small stab wounds. On the bed with the *disjecta membra* was the blade of a table-knife, the handle of which was found near the body wrapped in some underclothes. On the tallboy the police found a note: "This is the thing I thought would never come."

The victim of this appalling murder was a twenty-nine-year-old typist, Stephanie Baird. Miss Baird had chosen to live at the YWCA hostel because of its proximity to the Midland Nerve Hospital, where she was receiving regular treatment for recurring depression. She had planned to return to her home at Bishop's Cleeve, Gloucestershire, the following day.

Head of Birmingham CID, Chief Superintendent James Houghton, led the investigation. When pathologists and forensic experts had finished examining the body and the murder site, Houghton's team of detectives had little or nothing with which to start their enquiries. Of the murder itself, they learned that Stephanie Baird had died of strangulation but, aside from this fact, they knew no more. In the soft earth outside the Queen's Wing footprints were discovered but these impressions would only become significant if they could be matched with the shoes of the murderer. All the fingerprints found in Room No 4 were eliminated as belonging to the late occupant, her friends, or members of the hostel staff, leaving the police no nearer the suspect than when the murder was first discovered. The scribbled note, like the footprints, would only take on an importance if it could be linked to the killer.

As Margaret Brown had seen her attacker only briefly and in poor light, Superintendent Houghton realised that the value of her description was questionable. But this slim lead was all the police possessed. It was passed on to each officer manning roadblocks and checkpoints throughout the city and to those men making door-to-door enquiries in the immediate neighbourhood of the hostel. Within one minute of the report of an intruder, a patrol car had arrived at Wheeleys Road; within one hour of the call, the city of Birmingham was saturated with uniformed and plainclothes officers following a dozen different lines of investigation. Rapists, molesters and other known sexual offenders were questioned but all were soon eliminated. Detectives checked on local mental institutions to make sure no patients were absent without leave. Bus depots, railway stations and the airport were visited by police who interviewed workers and travellers, but no useful information emerged in the first few hours of the enquiry.

In fact, the case got off to an unfortunate start for Mr Houghton and his men with a misleading tip which wasted much valuable time and brought no rewards to the police for all their concentrated effort.

Mrs Peake, a publican's wife, told the police that sometime between 7.30p.m. and 8.00p.m. on 23 December, she had noticed a young man with blood on his hands and face leaning against a wall near the hostel. When asked if he was badly injured, he replied that he would be all right when he got home; he was just waiting for the next bus, he said. When a bus was stopped by police at a roadblock some distance from Edgbaston, the officers learned of a bloodstained man, whose description corresponded with that of the suspect. They became interested when they heard that he had entered the bus at Wheeleys Road, a short distance from the YWCA hostel. This information, together with the suspicious fact that blood was found on the floor of the upper deck, prompted detectives to take the bus off its route and have it driven to a municipal garage for a detailed examination. A thorough search of the vehicle produced no clues. The police, after further questioning, knew that the passenger they were seeking had left the bus at Hockley but, despite his bloodied condition and the intensive enquiries of a vast force of policemen who converged on the district, this man was never discovered.

This futile search was just one of many undertaken by the police during the course of their investigation into the YWCA hostel murder.

Because newspapers were not published over the Christmas holiday period, Chief Superintendent Houghton and his deputy, Detective Superintendent Gerry Baumber, had to bring news of the atrocity to the public's attention by other means. And it had to be done quickly, because they both knew that the man who had murdered one woman and made an attempt on the life of another was likely to strike again. While the man was still at large, he would remain a public menace.

All possible communications outlets were brought into use by the authorities. Saturday afternoon's televised sports programme was interrupted by Mr Houghton, who appealed to viewers to come forward with any information they might have on the crime, no matter how insignificant it might appear. The Lord Mayor of Birmingham also went on television to ask for the public's assistance. Radio broadcasts were made requesting listeners to cast their minds back to the night of the murder, with instructions to report to the police anything suspicious they might recall. Cinemas, dance-halls and football clubs were all involved in the appeal, with police-prepared scripts being read out to their patrons in a massive campaign designed to jog the memory of some member of the public who, the detectives believed, held vital information. The enormous indignation aroused by the murder and mutilation of Stephanie Baird was intensified, as Mr Houghton intended it should be, by the daily reporting of some aspect of the case in the newspapers, which had reappeared on 27 December.

The authorities were well aware that the case was an obvious lure for the unstable. The police request for assistance and the massive coverage given to the murder produced the usual crop of rumours, with some predictable results. As is usual with such a well-publicised crime, the police were submerged beneath an avalanche of confessions and solutions presented by an army of busybodies, cranks and the mentally disordered, some of them victims of morbid self-delusion who actually believed they had committed the murder. Others escaped from their lonely worlds to become the centre of attention in the temporary glare of sensational publicity. According to these and other informants, Birmingham seemed to be infested with bloodied strangers who appeared with the suddenness of apparitions and vanished just as quickly.

But every single statement had to be noted, checked and eliminated—a task requiring the attention of hundreds of police officers. As well as this waste of time and effort, the investigation was also hampered by the seasonal movement of the population which saw many citizens leave the city for a Christmas break, while others arrived in Birmingham to spend the holiday with family or friends.

The New Year arrived with Chief Superintendent Houghton and his men still baffled by the murder. Although standard police procedure had so far failed to unearth a solitary worthwhile clue, the investigators were convinced that the killer lived somewhere near to Wheeleys Road. Two reports of a peeping Tom seen months earlier at the hostel reinforced the view that the man they were looking for knew the general area and was familiar with the layout of the hostel buildings. In the light of this belief Houghton made a decision that could not have pleased his weary officers, already fighting the effects of boredom and fatigue.

One team of detectives who had previously questioned some 20 000 white male adults in the near neighbourhood of the hostel were directed to do so again. The movements of each individual interviewed were to be verified once more. While this task was being tackled, other squads of officers went to work re-checking hospital files for records of men attended to after 7.00p.m. on 23 December, all of whom were seen again and cleared. Surges of police activity were felt everywhere in the city. Shops, offices and factories were asked for lists of any employees who, without known reason, had failed to report to their place of work after Christmas. All of these men were discovered and questioned in locations as far apart as Cornwall and Co Durham before being dismissed from police consideration. When one of the pathologists assisting in the case, Dr Francis Camps, told the police that the body of the victim could not have been mutilated with the table-knife found at the scene, the investigation took on a new urgency and direction.

Because Dr Camps, a recognised authority in the field of criminal pathology, strongly maintained that the removal of the head would have required a much sharper implement which had probably been used by someone with butchery or medical skills, every butcher in the city had to account for his whereabouts on the night of 23 December. So also did hundreds of medical students. When their alibis were corroborated, all were excluded from further police investigation.

Despite these massive enquiries, the killer still eluded the investigators, but there were some compensations. So all-pervasive were the activities of the police that for seven weeks the city of Birmingham was almost totally free of crime.

The police had opened a detailed file for every man questioned since the beginning of the murder hunt, with a special staff employed to evaluate the information contained in the thousands of statements and completed questionnaires. Their analyses threw up a list of men who, although they had not been seen personally by an investigating officer, had for a variety of reasons been provisionally cleared of involvement in the death of Stephanie Baird. All but a few of these men had been followed-up and interviewed. One of those remaining to be interviewed was Patrick Joseph Byrne.

At the time of the murder, Byrne had been living at 97 Islington Row, not far from the YWCA hostel. On Christmas Eve, the day following the killing, he went to Lancashire. In ordinary circumstances, such a sudden move would have been viewed with suspicion. But there was nothing sudden or suspicious about Byrne's departure from Birmingham. In the early part of the month he had told his foreman that he would be leaving his job on 23 December. Mrs May Jeanes, his landlady, was also aware of Byrne's intention to visit his mother in Warrington, where, he told his fellow boarders, he intended to remain if he could find permanent work with a building company. These people also placed Byrne inside the lodging-house at the relevant time on the night of the murder. In their consideration of the case, the police did not think Patrick Byrne was a likely suspect, in view of the information that had come from these witnesses.

But now that a re-examination of the files had raised the name of Byrne, routine procedure required that he be interviewed. The police were anxious to hear what Byrne himself had to say about the night in question and to cross his name finally from the ever-decreasing list of those to be seen.

The police called again to Islington Row and got Byrne's address in Birchall Street, Warrington, Lancashire, which he had given to Mrs Jeanes.

A copy of the standard questionnaire used by the

Birmingham police in the Stephanie Baird enquiry was sent to the Warrington police, requesting them to have all queries answered by Byrne.

Patrick's mother, Mrs Elizabeth Byrne, who had recently moved her family from Dublin to Warrington, told the detective who called at her home that her son had come to see her at Christmas and, finding a suitable job in the town, had decided to stay. As Byrne was absent when the officer called, a message was left with his mother, asking that he visit Warrington police headquarters.

After seven weeks of exhaustive investigations, Birmingham city police were as mystified as they had been at the beginning of their massive man-hunt. Certainly, there was not the slightest reason to suspect Byrne. Nor was he under any suspicion whatsoever when, later the same day, 9 February 1960, he appeared as requested at the police station, where he was seen by Detective Sergeant George Welborn.

When the purpose of the interview was explained to him by the Warrington detective, Byrne answered questions clearly and without hesitation.

He gave his age as twenty-seven and said he was a Dublin man who had come to England when he was eighteen to join the British army. When he returned to civilian life, he remained in England, he said, working as a builder's labourer, most recently in and around Birmingham. On 23 December he had finished a job in that city, travelling the following day to his mother's home in Warrington, where he had since remained.

All his answers had been prompt, straightforward and unexceptional. Byrne's interview was over. But, with the well-developed instinct of the seasoned professional police officer, the sergeant thought he sensed a slight uneasiness in Patrick Byrne's manner and decided to ask him one last question. Was there anything else he would like to mention about his stay in Birmingham, Welborn enquired of Byrne. Byrne deliberated for a few moments and then answered: "I want to tell you about the YWCA. I have something to do with it."

Detective Sergeant Welborn tried to warn the man in front of him of the incriminating nature of his admission but there was no stopping Byrne. The dam had burst and words came tumbling from him as he was formally cautioned.

He could not sleep, he complained, although he had attempted to wipe the memory of the terrible event from his mind. It had been his intention to give himself up to the police even before he had been asked to visit the station. "The last seven weeks have been no good to me." He then made a short written statement which the Warrington police transmitted to their Birmingham colleagues.

As CS Houghton had already listened to and disposed of several spurious confessions, he could not discount the possibility that he was dealing with another hoaxer. He would remain unconvinced of the truth of these new disclosures until such time as he could interview the man who had made them.

Without delay, two CID officers drove north and brought Byrne back to Birmingham for further questioning.

With his deputy, Gerry Baumber, Chief Superintendent Houghton interviewed the prisoner and immediately it was established that Patrick Byrne was the YWCA murderer. In his many meetings with the press, Mr Houghton had asked journalists to refrain from divulging certain features of the murder as being too horrible for publication. Apart from the medical and forensic experts and a small number of police officers, only the killer of Stephanie Baird was aware of all the details of her death. Byrne knew everything there was to know about the killing.

The statement made by Byrne to the interrogating officers was long and detailed, and formed the basis of the Crown's argument when the case went to trial.

Byrne went to work as usual on 23 December. At about 1.00p.m. he left his job at the building site and went with some friends to the Ivy Bush public house on Hagley Road, where they stayed drinking until 3.00p.m. He returned to the site and climbed the scaffolding, only to be ordered back to the ground by the foreman, who considered him a danger to himself and to others. After collecting his money, he left the site for the last time. Wandering aimlessly home, he found himself near the YWCA hostel and, remembering previous occasions when he had looked into the girls' rooms, he decided to do so again. He entered the Queen's Wing through a passage window, and by standing on a chair, was able to look through a glass panel above cubicle No 4.

A woman who had been combing her hair opened the door as he was about to move away and asked him what he was doing. When he told her he was looking for someone, she said she would call the warden. Then he grabbed and kissed her; "She went backwards into the room with me squeezing her throat...as she fell she struck her head on the floor and...I was lying on top of her, kissing her." Describing his actions when he was certain she was dead, Byrne said he undressed the body and with only the small knife he had found in the room, he made numerous cuts in the upper and lower trunk before finally cutting off the head, which he examined closely before laying it on the bed.

The psychological drain on Byrne's mental resources must have been enormous, yet he said he was still in a very excited state and went looking for another woman to terrorise. His assault on Margaret Brown supports this claim: "I wanted to get my own back on them for causing me nervous tension through sex!"

Following the second attack, Byrne ran to his lodgings in Islington Row, a distance of 400 metres, where he changed his clothes immediately. Then he went to the bathroom and while washing himself stood before a mirror, "talking to myself and looking at my face for signs of a madman." He recalled the contents of a letter he had written to his landlady in which he referred to the killing at the hostel, blaming it on his split personality: "one very bad and the other the real me." But because he did not want to cause trouble for people at Christmas he had second thoughts about the letter, eventually tearing it up and dropping the pieces in the gutter.

Later the police would hear from several people who confirmed Byrne's belief in the duality of his character. His mother even thought she could explain its cause. According to Mrs Byrne, Patrick was her second child, born in Dublin in 1933. Although he remained at school until he was fourteen, he had always found difficulty in studying. She attributed his backwardness to an accident he suffered at the age of eight when part of a wall collapsed on him, leaving him with a broken leg and head injuries, which rendered him unconscious for seventy hours. She said he had become very introverted but, up to the time he left home to join the Royal Army Ordnance Corps, he had never caused her any trouble. The accident, she was sure, was the root of her son's problems.

Residents at the boarding house found Paddy Byrne, as he was called, a very quiet chap, seldom heard unless he had had a few drinks. Then he would sing but would stop as soon as anyone complained of the noise. His landlady, Mrs Jeanes, knew him as a thoughtful man and one easy to manage, and she, like almost everyone else who knew him, or thought they did, was astonished to hear of his arrest.

Another woman who made his acquaintance was Jean Grant, who met Byrne at a social club some months before the murder. She explained how, each evening they met at the club, she would have to lead him on to the floor because he was too shy to ask her to dance. He walked her home many nights, pointing out to her the dangers of walking home alone. He never did anything improper. "I just cannot understand how he did all those terrible things."

But there was evidence of a darker side to Byrne's nature. Two years earlier, in January 1958, he was sent to prison for two months for violently assaulting a policeman who was arresting him for being drunk and disorderly. Another report of the violence in Byrne's character was supplied by Michael Murphy, a friend of his, who had gone for a Christmas drink with him in Warrington. When the landlord of the Vine Hotel refused to serve him, Byrne affected a pugilistic pose and roared his intention of clearing the bar of all its customers. When he was again refused, despite his threats, Byrne said: "Give us the drinks or I'll knife you." It took the combined strength of four men to remove him from the premises. Although neither incident was sexually motivated, it did show evidence of Byrne's mental imbalance, which was to be exhaustively explored and analysed while he was waiting to stand trial for the killing of Stephanie Baird.

For years no murder trial in Britain had excited so much intense interest as did the hearing of the Patrick Byrne case, which was tried at Birmingham Assizes in March 1960, before Mr Justice Stable. Mr John Hobson QC led for the Crown, with Byrne's defence handled by Mr R Brown QC.

In a slight departure from established trial procedure, defence counsel addressed the court before the case for the prosecution had been presented. Brown told the jury that his client, who pleaded not guilty, would not be disputing the terrible facts of the crime. The defence would concern the condition of Byrne's mind at the time he murdered Miss Baird, and this was the issue the jurors would have to decide.

Before presenting the details of his case to the jury Hobson warned them that the prosecution's account of the death of Miss Baird would be more terrifying than anything they might experience in their worst nightmare. He agreed with defence counsel that their main consideration would centre on Byrne's mental condition at the time he killed his victim. Hobson then continued with his opening address.

A string of Crown witnesses were produced who testified to the accuracy of the facts as the prosecutor had outlined them, starting with the telephone report of the attack on Miss Margaret Brown—now Mrs Campbell—and closing with Patrick Byrne's statement to senior officers of

Birmingham city police.

Mrs Campbell repeated for the jury the story she had told the police of being struck on the head with a stone. Home Office pathologist Dr Frederick Griffiths confirmed the cause of Stephanie Baird's death as manual strangulation, as well as explaining about the extent of the body's mutilations. A cousin of the accused, Joseph Ryan, who also lodged with Mrs Jeanes, spoke of spending the night of 23 December drinking with Byrne, who seemed to be his usual calm self. (But Byrne was far from being his usual calm self. His outward poise was merely an act. In his statement to the police, Byrne told how he slept in his cousin's room when they returned from the pub because he was far too frightened to spend the night alone.) Evidence came next from Detective Sergeant Welborn, who related the details of the interview with the accused, while Chief Superintendent Houghton satisfied the court that there was no doubt about the prisoner being guilty, as he had particulars of the crime that only the killer could know.

All this testimony passed unchallenged and was followed by the evidence of the three medical experts called by the defence.

The first of these doctors to enter the witness-box was the Chief Medical Officer of Birmingham prisons, Dr Bray Coates. He said he considered the prisoner a sexual psychopath who derived satisfaction from the practice of perverted acts to such a marked degree that it had impaired his mental responsibility. He nurtured the delusion that he was thwarted in his sexual pursuits by young women who, he believed, would wish to have nothing to do with him except for the purpose of frustrating him. Although Byrne knew what he was doing was wrong, his sexual emotion had taken absolute control of his actions. When the judge asked if Byrne's behaviour was outside that of a normal human being, Dr Coates said it was.

Another doctor who had examined Byrne was Dr Joseph Reilly, lecturer in psychological medicine at Birmingham

University. According to Dr Reilly there was no doubt that Byrne was suffering from gross sexual abnormality. The doctor had reached this conclusion after listening to Byrne's history of dreams and fantasies, one of which involved pushing a woman through a circular saw. On the night of the murder, the doctor thought, Byrne's mind was so dominated by sexual fantasy that he was not only insensible to moral restraints but impervious to all considerations, even concern for his own safety. The doctor agreed that Byrne probably knew what he was doing was wrong but that a disease of the mind diminished his responsibility.

The last medical witness to testify, Dr Clifford Tellow, a psychologist at Central Hospital, Warwick, told Mr Justice Stable that Byrne was partly insane. The prisoner believed he was being watched by the police and the public while he murdered Miss Baird and this indicated to him, the doctor said, "that Byrne was abnormally excited sexually."

"That we have all grasped," observed the judge.

Addressing the jury on Byrne's behalf, Brown told them that if they accepted the sworn evidence of the medical gentlemen, they must bring in a verdict of not guilty of the charge of murder, but guilty of manslaughter.

In his closing speech for the Crown, Hobson reminded the jury, predictably, that all three medical experts had agreed that the accused man knew what he was doing was wrong at the time of killing. Only one verdict was possible under the law, Hobson said, guilty of murder.

Many explanations, some in direct conflict with each other, had been offered by the medical experts to account for Byrne's state of mind. He was a psychopath; he was insane—or partly so; he was overwhelmed by sexual emotion, reducing his powers of restraint. Yet in almost the same breath, the doctors admitted, in answer to specific questions put to them by the judge, that Byrne knew that he was doing wrong in murdering Stephanie Baird.

The jury, if confused, had their minds cleared for them by Justice Stables' summary of the evidence.

The judge instructed the jury to disregard sexual abnormality as being covered by the provisions of the Homicide Act 1957 (for the first time the act provided for a defence of diminished responsibility to the charge of murder). Sexual impulses, however forceful, did not amount to a mental abnormality that distorted the mind to such a degree as to absolve the prisoner of responsibility for the offence. They were not to interpret abnormal sexual drive as a form of mental disease. Such impulses were nothing more than lust. In other words, Byrne was depraved, not insane.

Left without choice by such judicial direction, the jury required only three-quarters of an hour to find Patrick Byrne guilty of murder.

He was sentenced to life imprisonment.

Although this verdict was altered to one of guilty of manslaughter, by a decision of the Court of Criminal Appeal in July 1960, the original sentence remained unchanged. The Lord Chief Justice, Lord Parker, said in handing down the court's ruling that, allowing for Byrne's tendencies, "he was what would be described in ordinary language as on the borderline of insanity." Few would disagree with that opinion.

In trying to capture the YWCA hostel murderer, the Birmingham police worked a seven-day, ninety-hour week. All leave and holidays were cancelled. A full-time force of 200 men was engaged exclusively on the case. To help him, the chief constables of seven other police authorities lent men to Chief Superintendent Houghton. In all, some 50 000 interviews were held and thousands of handwriting samples were examined for clues. Every police force in Britain cooperated and suspects were questioned in the Republic of Ireland. All British army personnel home from Europe on Christmas leave were traced and questioned—a slow task requiring the help of the army's Special Investigation Department—and every merchant seaman ashore in Birmingham at the relevant time was located and accounted for. Detectives even checked the names on library lists of those who had taken out a recently published book on "Jack the Ripper" in case the killer was among the borrowers.

Altogether, the investigation of the atrocity was a mammoth undertaking.

Yet, despite police persistence and the resourcefulness of its vast organisation, when Byrne called to Warrington police headquarters to answer questions from Sergeant Welborn, his appalling secret was still intact. Had he chosen not to confess, it is debatable whether Patrick Byrne would ever have been detected as the killer of Stephanie Baird.

Select Bibliography

Andrews, Allen, *Intensive Inquiries*, Harrap, London, 1973 (**Byrne**).

Bedford, Sybille, *The Best We Can Do*, Collins, London, 1958 (**Adams**)

Birkenhead, Earl of, *Famous Trials*, Hutchinson, London (no date) (**Burke and Hare**).

Bissitt, Ian, *Trial at Arms*, Panther, London, 1960 (**Emmett-Dunne.**)

Bolitho, William, *Murder for Profit*, Dobson, London, 1953 (**Burke and Hare**).

Camps, FE with Barber, Richard, *The Investigation of Murder*, Joseph, London, 1966.

Cassity, John Holland, *The Quality of Murder*, Julian Press, New York, 1958.

Casswell, JD, *A Lance for Liberty*, Harrap, London, 1960 (**Bryant**).

Cazauran, AR, *The Trial of Daniel McFarland*, Hilton, New York, 1870.

(No Author), *Crimes of Passion*, Treasure Press, London, 1985 (**Emmett-Dunne**).

Devlin, Patrick, *Easing the Passing*, Bodley Head, London, 1985 (**Adams**).

Douglas, Hugh, *Burke and Hare*, Hale, London, 1973.

Edwards, Owen Dudley, *Burke and Hare*, Polygon, Edinburgh (no date).

Firth, JB, *A Scientist Turns to Crime*, Wm Kimber, London, 1960 (**Clements**).

Furneaux, Rupert, *Famous Criminal Cases (6)*, Odhams, London, 1960 (**Byrne**).

Gaute, JHH and Odell, Robin, *Ladykillers*, Panther, London, 1980 (**Bryant, Webster**).

Glaister, John, *The Power of Poison*, Johnson, London, 1954.

Hallworth, Rodney and Williams, Mark, *Where There's a Will*, Capstan Press, Jersey, 1983 (**Adams**).

Huggett, Renee and Berry, Paul, *Daughters of Cain*, Allen and Unwin, London, 1956 (**Bryant**).

Hyde Montgomery, *Cases that Changed the Law*, Heinemann, London, 1951 (**Burke and Hare**).

Irving, HB, *A Book of Remarkable Criminals*, Cassell, London, 1918 (**Butler**).

Jackson, Robert, *Francis Camps*, Granada, London, 1983 (**Emmett-Dunne**).

Jones, Elwyn, *Death Trials*, Star, London, 1981 (**Adams**).

Lambert, Richard S, *When Justice Faltered*, Methuen, London, 1935 (**McFarland**).

Lindsay, Philip, *The Mainspring of Murder*, Long, London, 1958 (**Butler**).

Lucas, Norman, *The Sex Killers*, Allen, London, 1974 (**Byrne**).

Morland, Nigel, *Background to Murder*, Werner Laurie, London, 1955 (**Webster**).

Nice, Richard W (ed), *Crime and Insanity*, Philosophical Library, New York, 1958.

Notable British Trials series, William Hodge, Edinburgh and London (**Burke and Hare, Webster**).

Pakenham, Lord, *Causes of Crime*, Weidenfeld and Nicholson, London, 1958.

Simpson, Keith, *Forensic Medicine* (7th Ed), Arnold, London, 1974.

Yerrington, JMW, *The Trial of Sarah Jane Robinson*, Wright and Potter, Boston, 1888.

General Reference

Gaute, JHH and Odell, Robin, *Murder:"Whatdunnit,"* Harrap, London, 1982.

Gaute, JHH and Odell, Robin, *Murder:"Whereabouts,"* Harrap, London, 1982.

Gaute, JHH and Odell, Robin, *The Murderer's Who's Who*, Harrap, London, 1979.

Green, Jonathon, *The Directory of Infamy*, Mills and Boon, London, 1980.

Honeycombe, Gordon, *The Murders of the Black Museum*, Hutchinson, London, 1982.

Nash, Robert Jay, *Murder, America*, Harrap, London 1981.

Wilson, Colin and Pitman, Patricia, *Encyclopaedia of Murder*, Pan, London, 1984.